AIR FORCE GATOR
SCALES OF JUSTICE

by Dan Ryckert

FOREWORD
by That Idiot Jose Canseco

*Note from Dan Ryckert: As discussed with Mr.
Canseco, the following foreword is copied and
pasted directly from the text he sent me. He's a
really dumb guy, and I didn't want to take any
time editing his writing to make him look any
better.*

Air Force Gator is a thinly disguised
metaphorical depiction of my life. As you
remember from the first book, AFG was world
famous and legendary amongst his peers due to
his prowess achieved by taking the chemical
GatorAid, then fell into being shunned and
discarded by the world only to return in
triumphant vindication and once again take his
rightful place as a saviour of humanity. Sound
familiar? Gatoraid -- Steroids. Famous and
legendary -- that was me. Shunned and
blackballed -- that's what MLB did to me. An evil
nemesis Gustav -- that's Bud Selig. Vindicated
and Triumphant -- again me as I turned out to
be the only one telling the truth about the
Steroid Era and ended up saving baseball. It was
unauthorized and weakly veiled but we all know
what Dan was doing here.
Air Force Gator II, or whatever the hell
Dan is calling this sequel, continues the
chronicling of my resurrection in society and the
good that I am able to do for all. There are more
assumptions made in this book as it is not as

anthropomorphically historical as AFG I but is a highly probable prediction of the things I will be able to accomplish. Kind of a tome of reptilian based Nostradamus Canseco prophecies. The writing is mediocre and the plot development is a bit pedestrian for my taste, but read with the knowledge that this is really about Jose Canseco will keep you turning its pages late into the night. It's like Sid Meier's Civilization or eating popcorn in that you know it's really not that good for you but you just can't stop.

      Dan's future as a writer is uncertain so enjoy this literary effort as there may not be a lot of Ryckert publications to fill up your kindle in the future. I will tell you this though, that without Dan Ryckert the story of Air Force Gator never would have been told.

hug for u,

Jose Canseco #33

Prologue

On a March morning in 2005, Air Force Gator successfully thwarted the terrorist plot of his former partner, the evil crocodile Gustav Leonidas. With the malevolent crocodile's body blown to pieces and his base burning at the bottom of the ocean, the homeland never had to face the devastating effects of his impending biological attack. A direct assault on America was avoided, but Air Force Gator's explosive assault led to unforeseen consequences that would alter the course of the country's history.

Tens of thousands of gallons of the chemical GatorAid were housed in rows of chemical vats on Crocodile Rock. Air Force Gator's bombs killed Gustav's men and destroyed his Croc Flock, but the base's GatorAid supply was blown into the Gulf of Mexico. Neon orange water stretched out in a half-mile radius surrounding the wreckage of Crocodile Rock. Hundreds of sea creatures perished in the contaminated waters, but one group of reptiles survived and grew stronger than ever.

Gustav's GatorAid research program housed nearly one hundred crocodiles and alligators in the labs of Crocodile Rock. Many of them perished during Air Force Gator's attack, but a group of over forty reptiles was blown free from their cages and rejuvenated in the same water that killed so much sea life. Before they landed in the gulf, these crocodiles and alligators were bloody and bruised, many missing limbs. Within minutes, they resurfaced stronger than ever and fully intact. GatorAid flowing through their veins, these creatures were confused and fascinated by their newfound strength.

Most of the reptiles were busy flexing and staring at their new muscles as they treaded water, but one alligator began to notice the GatorAid's psychological effects. Sentient for the first time in his existence, this alligator became aware that something monumental was happening inside of him. In time, he would become the defacto leader of this group of mutated reptiles. At that moment, however, he was simply concerned with getting his fellow creatures to safety. Not yet understanding the English language, the alligator began to loudly yell and wave his arms to draw the attention of the rest. Once he had their attention, he led the group in swimming to the nearest land - the swamps of Louisiana.

Attacked by a shark at a young age, a long scar ran across this alligator's face. Combined with body-length burn scars from the explosions at Crocodile Rock, his appearance was at odds with the brilliant tiny alligator brain housed in his elongated skull.

This scarred alligator was the first to rise to his hind legs on the shores of Lake Tambour. Soon after, over forty of his fellow creatures rose alongside him. One confused box turtle stood among the alligators and crocodiles, as he had been doused in GatorAid while swimming near Crocodile Rock at the time of the blast. He was blissfully unaware of the experiments being performed on reptiles at the base, but the chemical affected him just the same once it spilled into the gulf.

For weeks, the reptiles camped out near Lake Tambour as they struggled to comprehend the changes their minds and bodies were going through. Fascinated by their new strength, many of them passed the days by performing hundreds of push-ups. Others used branches on nearby trees as pull-up bars. It resembled a prison courtyard, with the reptiles having nothing better to do with their time than maintaining their artificially-improved physiques.

While the rest of the reptile crew mindlessly compared their biceps and got into fights, the scarred leader spent his time deep in thought. He frequently drew pictures in the sand with a stick, recreating his disturbing memories from Air Force Gator's assault on Crocodile Rock. Other reptiles began to crowd around the leader as he drew pictures and struggled to communicate via grunts and growls.

After two months of occupying the area surrounding the lake, the leader grew restless. He began to suspect that there was a world far more complex than any he had seen in his short life, and this feeling was confirmed when he spotted his first airplane. Already tired of his group's tiresome daily routine at the lake, he began growling and waving his arms just as he had done in the waters surrounding Crocodile Rock. Once the rest of the reptiles had crowded around him, he gestured for the group to follow him into uncharted territory.

Not one of the reptiles in the group knew what their final destination was, not even the scarred leader. Trailing behind the company was the box turtle, struggling to keep up thanks to his little turtle legs. Days of marching would go by without any sign of progress, but every once in a while the group would spot something that restored their focus. Planes continued to fly overhead. Cars could be heard on distant highways. These events didn't make the world any less confusing to the reptiles, but they served as reminders that there was something beyond the swamp.

Many of the reptiles were tiring after two weeks of walking, but their faith was restored on one particular afternoon. They encountered a dirt road that led through the woods, and followed it until they noticed a driveway extending into the foliage. Walking down the short path, they suddenly found themselves standing in front of a one-story wooden lakehouse. Confused by the discovery, the group began growling and yelling until the front door opened.

A large, white-bearded man in his fifties stood in the doorway with a shotgun.

"The fuck are y'all doin' in front of my house?" he asked.

A smattering of confused grunts came from the reptiles as they looked back and forth at each other. Being subjected to experiments on Crocodile Rock was their only previous interaction with humans, but any recollection of those days was a distant memory to their little reptilian brains.

"Listen here and listen good, you sonsabitches," the bearded man said. "I don't trust a single one of your kind ever since that mean-ass croc tried that bullshit back in '05. Y'all got ten seconds to git on back to whence you came, else you want your slimy asses to be filled with buckshot, ya hear?"

Unaware of the danger they were in and unable to communicate, the reptile crew shuffled about and stared at birds. The only member of the group to pay any mind to the homeowner was the scarred leader. He stared into the bearded man's eyes as he continued to count backward.

"5...4...3..."

While the alligator couldn't understand the man's words, he was perceptive enough to detect the hate in his eyes. His alligator brain didn't know what to expect, but he began to worry. The turtle also seemed to pick up on the unsettling vibe in the air, retreating into his shell.

"2...1..." continued the man. "Zero. You dumb reptile motherfuckers can't even wise up when you got a Remington in your face. Now y'all gonna make me dirty my front deck with gator blood."

With that, the man fired his shotgun into the group of reptiles. Several were hit with buckshot and stumbled into the woods. Others covered their ears and fell to the ground as the man reloaded. Reptile blood painted the ground as another blast rocked the group.

Acting on self preservation, the scarred leader charged the bearded man. Ripping the shotgun from his hands, the alligator snapped it in two across his massive knee.

"Whoa whoa whoa, you back the fuck up you dirty reptile," the man said nervously. "I gave y'all a chance, just back up now and you won't see no more of your buddies' cold blood spillin' on the floor. Don't you go and make me call the sheriff, now."

Grabbing the stock end of the shotgun, the alligator leader swung it and cracked the bearded man across the temple. As the man crawled towards his front door in a daze, the alligator bent down and sank his teeth into his forehead. With one sharp motion, the alligator jerked his head back and removed the entirety of the man's face, beard and all. Eyes, teeth, muscle, and blood were all that remained of the screaming face as he convulsed on the ground.

Injured reptiles began to slowly return from the woods, watching their leader as he towered above the human who attacked them mere moments earlier. The turtle slowly peeked out of his shell to witness the encounter.

Raising his scarred, massive foot in the air, the alligator stared down at the bloody mess below him. With a thundering stomp, the gigantic foot came crashing down, decimating the man's skull beneath it. Brain matter and skull fragments were driven deep into the wooden deck as the alligator grinded his foot into the ground.

A moment of stunned silence passed before the reptiles began pumping their fists in the air, bursting into a chorus of cheerful grunts and the occasional turtle squeak. Their scarred leader stood on the deck above the man's corpse and raised his fists high above him. Once the celebration began to subside, the group was waved into the house by the dominant alligator.

They had never been inside a house, but it didn't take long for the reptiles to get comfortable. Some sprawled out on the house's bed and couches. Others rifled through the refrigerator and cupboard, inhaling entire raw steaks, sticks of string cheese, and bags of Combos.

In the weeks to come, this modest swamp house became the home of the reptiles' first real education. It didn't take long for the group to learn how to use forks and knives, but more advanced tools and technology took them longer to grasp. The home featured an active internet connection, but the crocodiles and alligators struggled with the concept of a computer mouse, and their lack of fluency in the English language made web browsing difficult.

No genuine learning materials could be found in the house, but their leader became obsessed with accumulating knowledge in any way possible. He didn't know how to swap out DVDs, but he repeatedly watched the copy of *Tango & Cash* that the owner had been watching when they initially arrived. The bearded man was far from well-read, but the copies of *Hustler* and *Field & Stream* strewn about the house gave the scarred alligator something to practice reading on.

It was a slow process, but the leader eventually learned enough of the language for basic communication. His fellow reptiles didn't catch on as easily, but they began to understand basic commands from their leader. Once he felt that he had utilized all materials in the house to the fullest, the alligator decided it was time to move on.

"Follow!" barked the alligator leader one morning. Combined with his gesture, the rest of the group knew it was time to move out. They stuffed whatever magazines and remaining food that they could find into the bearded man's backpack and grocery bags, and moved out of the wooden shack.

Continuing their journey north, the entire group was far more prepared to evolve as a species. They entered the house as ignorant, violent animals. When they left, the combination of the GatorAid's effects and their findings from the house led to an intellectual curiosity that was completely absent when they first left Crocodile Rock.

When they first saw the city of New Orleans on the horizon, they were ready to explore the modern world and become educated members of society. Their good intentions weren't enough, however, as the city (and country) wasn't ready for the imminent and irreversible change these reptiles would bring.

DAN RYCKERT

Chapter I

July 10, 2012

New Orleans, Louisiana

Seven years have passed since the events of Crocodile Rock. Seven years since Air Force Gator's assault set events in motion that led to the creation of that mutated group of reptiles. In the years that followed, the group tried desperately to conform to American society. These 42 creatures moved into apartments in the same low-income area of New Orleans, working jobs as Walmart cashiers, gas station attendants, and elementary school janitors. Even their gifted leader was relegated to a position selling pull tabs at a local dive bar.

Three, four, sometimes five of these reptiles were crammed into a single studio apartment. They had arrived almost a decade ago with the most innocent of intentions, but the shadow of Gustav's terrorist actions on Crocodile Rock followed them everywhere. Most of the group had become fluent in English, yet finding work was a constant struggle. A large majority of Americans had no experience in reptile relations outside of what the news reported regarding the attempted biological attack in 2005. Reptiles were vilified and ostracized, and this group from the waters of the Gulf of Mexico had all but given up.

Most of the crocodiles and alligators were working their second or third shifts of the day when the number 17 bus rolled into town. None of them saw the man from Tennessee exit the vehicle, chewing on a piece of hay. Knapsack over his shoulder, Dennis Godwinn wore his trademark overalls over a weathered yellow flannel shirt. Distinct white mutton chops stretched across his cheeks as a straw hat cast a shadow over his face.

It was his first time visiting this poor area of New Orleans, but the man had done his research. He had kept a keen eye on the plight of the reptile ever since the Crocodile Rock incident. Where the reptiles saw struggle and hardship, Godwinn saw opportunity. Back in Tennessee, he had managed to accumulate a small fortune thanks to his pig farm and wise investment decisions. Arriving in New Orleans, he was confident that his new plan would work in his favor just like every other event in his life.

Finding places to stay or jobs to apply for wasn't on his mind in these first hours. Instead, he reached into his knapsack and immediately went to work. Hundreds of fliers were packed into his bag, and they were specifically created to speak directly to the disenfranchised reptiles of New Orleans.

"*This is not your American Dream*," read the fliers, the text positioned over a picture of an alligator assembling an Egg McMuffin. "*This is not what you were promised. You deserve more.*

Change your destiny...9pm Friday at Gretna Bingo Palace."

Godwinn had ensured that the bingo hall would be a private affair, allowing admission only the reptile population with whom he wished to speak. With a nearly endless supply of funds, it wasn't hard for the Tennessee pig farmer to get what he wanted. His fliers were posted on every street light, stop sign, and bulletin board in the reptilian part of town, and he had inserted additional information in the mailboxes of every confirmed reptile residence in the area. A good turnout wasn't guaranteed for Godwinn's event, but fate tended to smile upon the blue collar genius.

As the pig farmer walked from corner to corner stapling fliers to posts, the scarred alligator leader spotted him late at night on his way home from working the bar. Godwinn was ready to retire for the night, and began walking to the nearest hotel. Before he could arrive at a bed and much-needed sleep, he felt a scaly claw grip his left shoulder.

"What do you want from us?" the voice asked.

Godwinn turned around and saw the scarred alligator snout staring back at him.

"Brother, I ain't here to ask anything from you," Godwinn said. "I don't want no money from y'all, 'cause I know you don't got it. And that's a damn crime if you ask me. I came to town to help y'all get what you deserve."

"What would that be?" the alligator asked.

"Justice, my new friend. None of y'all done a damn thing wrong since you been here, and it's gettin' near ten years. You ask me, I say you all got reason to be madder than a box of frogs."

"None of us are where we want to be," the alligator said. "But you'll have to forgive me if I wonder how a straw-hatted son of a bitch human knows how to get us what we deserve."

"Don't eye me wrong 'cause I'm a human, brother. I'm on your side, and y'all gonna like what I got to say this Friday. You rally those cold-blooded buddies of yours, and I'll tell you everything you need to hear."

The alligator leader stared at Godwinn, a clear distrust in his eyes.

"I don't blame you for givin' me that look," said Godwinn. "But bring your buddies and keep those tiny brains open. Right now, y'all don't even got names. By the time we leave that bingo hall this weekend, you all gonna have names and a purpose. You can take that to the bank, new friend."

Even without a clear statement of purpose, the alligator leader could sense a fire in the pig farmer's eyes. This man meant what he said, and the alligator was smart enough to acknowledge that the reptile cause was being held back thanks to the actions of the evil crocodile Gustav back in 2005. Perhaps a passionate new face was what it would take to light a fire under the ass of the movement, even if that face belonged to a human.

"You've got a tough sell ahead of you," said the alligator. "But you've got my attention. I'll spread the word, and you'll have your audience. You fuck this up, and my boys will drive you out of town just as fast as you got here."

"By the time I'm done talkin' at that bingo hall, y'all gonna be begging me for your first order. You crocs and gators want what you don't have, but you don't have the smarts yet to make it happen. I got those smarts, and I'm gonna give you all the tools you need to get what's comin' to you."

Godwinn and the scarred alligator exchanged a firm handshake and went their separate ways for the night. With no formal education and limited exposure to humans, the alligator was unsure of how much faith to put in the pig farmer. Regardless, it was the first whiff of potential progress in quite some time. He'd hear out the human on Friday night, but he didn't have the slightest idea what to expect.

July 13, 2012

Forty-two reptiles shifted uncomfortably in their plastic chairs at the Gretna Bingo Palace in New Orleans. Their alligator leader sat at the front of the room, checking the clock on the wall in anticipation for the 9pm start time. He was intrigued by the pig farmer's vague statements, but didn't know what to expect from his reptile cohorts when a human stepped up to the microphone.

"Why we here, boss?" one crocodile yelled from the crowd.

"I don't know much more than any of you," said the scarred gator. "Sit tight and we'll all learn together. I've got a feeling that this might be a good thing for all of us."

Crocodiles, alligators, and the one turtle grew restless as the minutes crept past nine o'clock. Shots were ordered, alligators crowded around the jukebox, and a crocodile began singing karaoke as the group seemingly forgot about the reason they had gathered on this Friday night. Suddenly, the karaoke audio was cut off and the reptiles turned towards the front of the room.

"I hope I'm not interruptin' this night of spirits and troublemakin', but I got something to say that y'all might want to hear," said a voice from the bingo hall's speakers.

"Sit down," the scarred alligator said firmly. "All of you."

"I'm 'bout to walk out there in front of y'all, and it ain't gonna be what you expect," continued the voice. "I just ask that you listen to what I got to say rather than how I look. I'm here for you 'cause you got the short end of the stick in these last few years."

As the voice continued, the source of it emerged from behind the bar. Large, tooth-lined jaws dropped and crocodile eyes peeked up over their glasses as Dennis Godwinn walked confidently with microphone in hand. Most in attendance felt they had been duped, as humans typically avoided any contact with these refugees from Crocodile Rock.

"I can see in most of y'alls beady little reptile eyes that you don't trust me, and I understand that," said Godwinn as he made his way to the front of the bingo hall. "You all are probably used to humans leaving the damn room when you step in, but that ain't me. I grew up on my daddy's pig farm in Tennessee, but truth be told it wasn't for me. Naw, what I really cared about was your kind. All the other kids at school had farmers for daddies and tended to the livestock. Me, I just wanted to take care of my pet snakes. Those kids called me an odd duck and made funna me, but I didn't care none. I knew what I cared about, and it was your kind"

He had the attention of the crowd at the Bingo Palace, but they remained skeptical of his intentions. Other humans had tried to exploit the reptiles for political or personal gain in the years since they arrived, and they had learned to distrust mankind.

"Bein' the reptile-lovin' kid that I was, you can imagine how I felt when I heard about that croc Gustav and what he did out there in the ocean. Finally, I saw someone with a brain like mine. Someone that wanted reptiles to get what was comin' to them. He wanted a reptile in the White House, he wanted little baby turtles and snakes to share daycares with baby humans, he wanted a gator to have the right to marry a nice

17

human lady. And what did he get for his vision? He had one of his own kind fly a goddamn aeroplane over his home and kill him dead."

Skepticism began to turn to anger amongst the crowd as they were reminded of Air Force Gator's actions back in 2005.

"The croc that I saw as a hero got killed for fighting for what he thought was right. Then I heard about y'all washin' up here in N'awlins. Gustav may be dead, but by God, look what we got here now. We got 42 reptiles in this room, and y'all smart as fuck thanks to that GatorAid mess. All you boys need is a leader, someone to help you tip the scales of justice back towards our side. When I heard about that brilliant croc dyin', I knew I had to move down here so I could rub shoulders with your kind. I'm gonna be that leader that y'all need."

He was quickly winning the reptiles over, with raised eyebrows and suspicious stares being replaced with bursts of applause.

"Gustav was a visionary, but his plan was flawed. We don't need to be spendin' our time worryin' about evolving our species with some chemical anymore. You all got smart brains now, and your kids'll have that too. What we need to worry about is the other part of Gustav's plan...takin' out those human sons of bitches that have been holdin' you down all these years!"

Scaly arms rose into the air as every reptile in the Bingo Palace erupted into cheers.

"Today is the day we start to fight back! I want every single one of y'all standin' with me, and we're gonna stick it to those god damn humans! You and me, we ain't just a bunch of reptiles and a pig farmer. From now on, we're the Sons of Gustav. And it's about time y'all had names. Lookin' around this room, I count 42 folks including myself. What a nice coincidence, my reptile brothers. I say we each get us a downright presidential namesake. Forget my ol' family name, 'cause I don't give a shit about those Godwinn hillbillies. You can all call me Van Buren. Hell, I already got these big-ass white chops on my face."

The reptiles laughed.

"You! Big man with the scars!" said Van Buren as he pointed to the alligator leader. "You're Pierce now."

Smiling, the scarred alligator nodded.

"And you, turtle boy! You're Monroe."

Van Buren walked from table to table with microphone in hand, assigning each reptile their new moniker. For the first time since they arrived on the shores of Lake Tambour, the reptiles felt like they had a purpose. This eccentric pig farmer from Tennessee had managed to win them over within twenty minutes of meeting them, and the Sons of Gustav were born.

Round after round of beers and shots were bought by the charismatic human, but the good times would soon give way to nefarious plans. Tonight was a night for mirth and merriment, but the plot to devastate the human race would soon be on the table.

DAN RYCKERT

Chapter 2

March 25, 2013

Washington, D.C.

On this gorgeous spring day, a crowd of over 200,000 proud Americans packed the National Mall. From the Washington Monument to the Lincoln Memorial, the buzzing attendees anxiously awaited an increasingly rare public appearance from the nation's hero. Today was the eighth anniversary of the attempted attack on America emanating from Crocodile Rock. In honor of one heroic alligator's actions on that day, President Obama was set to announce a new national holiday...Air Force Gator Day.

It was a reason to celebrate, but each and every member of the crowd was all too aware of the elephant in the room. Air Force Gator had saved the United States from a terrifying future, but he inadvertently set into motion one of the most controversial eras in modern history. The Sons of Gustav were a small group that was rarely spotted outside of New Orleans, but the entire nation knew of their plight.

This vocal minority of reptiles had become increasingly bitter over the years, even with their successful attempts at gaining wealth and education. With the guidance of their human leader Van Buren, these crocodiles and alligators were frequently discussed on a national scale.

21

Van Buren was now a fixture on cable news programs, often delivering impassioned, charismatic rants about the injustice his reptile followers faced on a daily basis.

Many found his wide-eyed sermons unsettling, and others were correct in their assumptions that the Sons of Gustav were participating in activities of questionable legality. A small group of four crocodiles maintained a successful email scam. Monroe the turtle used underground connections to bring significant cash flow to the Sons via insider trading. Van Buren improvised military training for the group by feeding the reptiles a daily diet of *Commando* and *Windtalkers* viewings. Most of the group was making cash for the Sons via shady scams, but the more brazen alligators and crocodiles donned masks and robbed local banks for quick cash.

In the eight years since the Sons of Gustav stood up on dry land for the first time, they had grown into a veritable criminal empire. They had arrived with benevolent intentions, but were greeted by a prejudiced and terrified population. Shaken by the Crocodile Rock incident, most American citizens viewed any reptile as an enemy. Perhaps they would have quietly lived their lives in New Orleans if it weren't for Van Buren's involvement. In the eight months since their human leader stepped off the bus in New Orleans, they had grown from a disenfranchised group of mutants to a deadly force with more money than they knew how to spend.

These Sons of Gustav were the spectre that hung over this day on the National Mall. At an event that was meant to celebrate one alligator's heroic accomplishments, everyone in attendance knew the challenges the nation was facing and often ignoring. Despite Van Buren's constant pleas to cable news, state senators, and the internet, no one outside of the Sons had legitimately spoken up about the nation's path in terms of reptile rights.

If there was ever a day to start the national conversation, it was today. President Obama was set to introduce Air Force Gator on the steps of the Lincoln Memorial, and the press was buzzing about a long-awaited statement regarding the place of reptiles in the country's future.

The president was set to appear at any minute. On the steps of the memorial was a podium flanked by ZZ Top, who were providing the pre-speech entertainment at Air Force Gator's personal request. As Billy Gibbons and Dusty Hill played through "Pearl Necklace," the crowd eagerly anticipated the imminent appearance of President Obama and America's hero alligator.

After an extended solo and a couple of fuzzy guitar spins, ZZ Top ended their celebratory set. Billy Gibbons smiled and approached the podium.

"Ladies and gentlemen, it's been a pleasure performin' for you on this special day," Gibbons said. "But today ain't about us. It's about celebrating the men and women that allow us to keep living free and kickin' ass. Right now, I want to introduce the leader of the greatest country in the world, our commander in chief, and if we must say so ourselves...one hell of a sharp dressed man."

The crowd laughed.

"Let us see your hands and hear your voices for President Barack Obama!"

Applause filled the National Mall as the 44th President of the United States made his entrance to the unmistakable riffs of the 1983 hit that Gibbons had alluded to. He waved to the mass of citizens before shaking the hands of ZZ Top and joining them for a photo op, performing their trademark "spinning point" gesture.

"Thank you. Thank you," said the president as he attempted to quiet the crowd. "My fellow Americans, we are here today to celebrate one of our nation's greatest heroes. Every man, woman, and child standing with me here in Washington or watching from home knows about the sacrifice and struggle of one extraordinary alligator eight years ago today. Because of his bravery on that March morning, I declare March 25th to forever be known as our newest national holiday, Air Force Gator Day."

Members of the crowd held up Air Force Gator signs as they cheered the official announcement.

"While this day is born out of celebration, let us not turn a blind eye to the struggles that have faced our nation ever since that fateful morning in 2005. Ever since Air Force Gator thwarted the plans of a vindictive, hateful crocodile, we've encountered prejudice and bigotry in this nation not seen for decades. Innocent reptiles have migrated to our shores in search of the American Dream, and they've been met with undue hostility.

Let us not forget that we are Americans. We as a nation have overcome so much in such a short amount of time. We've stood for what is right and realized the error of discrimination based on gender, race, ethnicity, and sexual orientation. These reptiles are no different than the trailblazers that fought for the rights of Americans for the last century. It's true that a terrible plot was hatched against the American people back in 2005, but I ask that we as a people do not allow the sins of one crocodile to prevent a generation of reptiles from participating in the pursuit of happiness that our nation promised in 1776. I ask that we as Americans choose to embrace rather than shun, to offer opportunity rather than prejudice. We've grown too much as a nation to drive rightful U.S. citizens to the fringes of society."

As Obama continued his speech, a considerably more low-key conversation was taking place behind him in the Lincoln Memorial. A massive American flag obscured the iconic statue of our 16th president, where two folding chairs sat at his marble feet.

In one chair sat the nation's Vice President.

"Sounds like a big crowd out there, buddy. How come you don't seem more nervous?," Joe Biden asked as he finished the ass end of his 40-ounce bottle of Mickey's malt liquor. "Must take a lot to rattle your scaly ass, you tough son of a bitch."

Across from him sat the massive figure of a legend. The battle-scarred alligator leaned back in his metal folding chair, trademark goggles strapped across his forehead and empty cans of Milwaukee's Best scattered around his clawed feet.

"Joe, I've killed thousands of people," Air Force Gator said. "I ripped the dick off of the most notorious terrorist in the world. I watched my mentor get eaten by an asshole crocodile. I've been bathed in the blood and entrails of my former partner. You think I get nervous about a couple hundred thousand Americans that showed up here to metaphorically suck my scaly dick? Not a chance."

"I'm sure you're gonna get in the pants of one of those pretty ones, you shady son of a bitch." the Vice President said.

"Nah. The old Air Force Gator would be balls deep in strange cooze tonight, but my hot stripper girlfriend takes good care of this old horndog."

"Is that right? Didn't know you were a domesticated breed these days."

"My years of getting high and banging whores next to the interstate are over, Joe. I knew Trish was the one for me ever since I felt those big, tan titties bounce across my snout at the Shady Lady."

"Well good for you, ya lucky son of a bitch," the Vice President said as he heard the crowd begin to stir on the other side of the flag. "Sounds like they're getting ready for you out there, buddy. Better kill that last one."

Air Force Gator casually tossed his fifteenth can of Milwaukee's Best into his mouth and crushed it between his vice-like jaws.

"Still doing that old party trick," the Vice President said. "Quit showing off and get out there."

With a smile, Air Force Gator belched and stepped over empty cans on his way towards the people. He heard the president's voice echo out over the crowd.

"My fellow Americans, please welcome the man of the hour. Air Force Gator!"

A roar rose above the National Mall, and Air Force Gator's ovation could be heard all the way from the Lincoln Memorial to the Capitol steps. Tens of thousands of dollars worth of fireworks exploded above the proceedings as the alligator stepped out from behind the gigantic American flag. Standing over eight feet tall ever since being exposed to GatorAid, the national hero walked towards the podium. President Obama reached his hand out, which was met with a scaly, strong grip. After shaking hands, Air Force Gator offered the Commander in Chief a sharp salute, then turned to the crowd.

It was a scene reminiscent of The Beatles

on *The Ed Sullivan Show.* Women pulled at their hair and shrieked as men loudly applauded, some with tears running down their face. For several minutes, Air Force Gator posed and flexed as the mass of Americans grew louder and louder. At one point, he grabbed Secretary of State John Kerry and began repeatedly pressing him over his head. Kerry laughed until his stomach hurt as the crowd ate up every second of it.

Setting down the Secretary of State, Gator approached the podium.

"Alright, alright," he said, attempting to calm the frenzied crowd. "Don't shit your pants, people. You're acting like you've never seen a fucking alligator before."

Smiling at Gator's trademark inelegance, the crowd politely hushed.

"Man, this is weird as shit. It wasn't that long ago that I was paying tubby, weird-lookin' hookers to touch my dick. Now look at that!"

Air Force Gator pointed towards Trish, his hot stripper girlfriend that was standing on the side of the stage. She let out an enthused yell as she raised her tank top and shook her giant, tanned breasts to the delight of the crowd.

"Fuck, I'll never get tired of those cans," Air Force Gator said. "Don't tire yourself out shaking those, baby. I'm going to town on you tonight."

Trish blew Gator a kiss and mimicked an oral sex motion as the crowd cheered wildly.

"Great, now I gotta finish this stupid speech while those awesome titties are fresh in my mind. Anyways, I really do think it's cool that all of you showed up here today. I'm just an alligator that's good at flying airplanes. Back in my days at the academy, I would have thought you were crazy if you told me that I'd be getting my own national holiday from the president himself. And on that note, don't turn Air Force Gator Day some stupid fucking thing where you just put out a flag and call it a day. I want New Year's and St. Patty's to look like a trip to the old folk's home compared to this holiday. All of you are getting fucked up every AFG Day, and you're a fucking pussy if you don't."

Another wave of cheers was offered from the crowd as they nodded in agreement. Near the front of the crowd stood the evil pig farmer Van Buren and Monroe the turtle.

"Listen close, turtle," Van Buren said as he crouched down to reach Monroe's ear. "When shit goes down tonight, don't forget your job. We're all hightailing it out of this country, but you stay right here and be my eyes and ears in the homeland. You tip me off ASAP if you think that gatah catches wind of where we're goin'."

Monroe nodded his little turtle head as Van Buren grabbed a megaphone and began working his way towards the Lincoln Memorial.

"It's been a great eight years, people," Air Force Gator continued. "Ever since I killed the shit out of that asshole Gustav, it's been pretty smooth sailing. I flew some sorties, killed a shit ton more terrorists, and fell in love. Looking over there at Trish, I don't think there's anything in the world that would make me happier than spending the rest of my life getting drunk and banging her back in New Orleans."

Whispers began running through the crowd, with many nervously anticipating an unexpected retirement announcement.

"I guess what I'm trying to say is, it's time for me to hang up my boots."

Shrieks and sobs immediately sprang from the crowd, with several teenage girls falling to the floor in anguish.

"I know, I know. It must have been pretty cool for all of you to see the news and hear about an alligator killing a bunch of al Qaeda shitheels, but I've accomplished everything I set out to do. All of their leaders are dead, and the only terrorists that are left are a bunch of Richard Reid dipshits that don't know a suicide vest from a sweater vest. We've got the best military in the world, and they're more than equipped to deal with these limp-dicked wannabes. This country is safe now, and it's time for me to officially announce..."

Before Air Force Gator could finish his speech, a voice rang out through the crowd.

"Hold on there, Gatah!" said an amplified voice. Looking around, the crowd saw a man with white-whiskers, a straw hat, and overalls make his way towards the podium with a megaphone. It was Van Buren. Pushing through the crowd, Secret Service officers quickly made their way towards him.

"Wait a second, boys," Air Force Gator said. "Let's hear what this scraggly-ass piece of trash has to say."

Van Buren stared down the agents as he stepped onto the stage, then turned his attention to the alligator at the podium.

"Oh I'm the piece of trash, am I Gatah?" Van Buren said. "Last I checked, you were nothing but a coward, a hypocrite, and a traitor to your own kind."

"The fuck are you talking about, you Hee Haw-looking son of a bitch?" Air Force Gator asked.

"Look at why these folks are here today. They're celebratin' the fact that you killed the one crocodile that was fighting for his kind. Reptiles were ready to take their rightful place in this country, and you had to go and put a grenade down his gullet."

"He was going to kill innocent Americans, you dumbass."

"But he had a purpose!" Van Buren yelled, his face becoming red. "Reptiles wouldn't be in the shitty-ass situation they're in now if you'd have let him help. He wanted the best for his kind, for *your* kind, and you had to stop him. I bet he's spinnin' in his grave right now because of what's transpired in the last eight years."

"He's not in a grave, idiot. I blew him the fuck up."

"Regardless, you're a traitor to your own kind. Here you are posing for photos while reptiles still can't get a damn job. And now you're ready to just fly off into the sunset and pretend like you've made this country a better place. Makes me sick."

Air Force Gator grabbed the microphone and walked towards Van Buren. Pressing his snout against the whiskered man's nose, he spoke forcefully and deliberately.

"My days of putting up with assholes ended when I felt Gustav's cold blood rain down on my head. I'm fucking done with this."

Headbutting Van Buren off of the stage, Gator retreated back towards the Lincoln Memorial. With the crowd in a nervous fervor, a bleeding Van Buren grabbed his megaphone and regained his footing.

"There's your fuckin' hero, America!" he shrieked into the megaphone. "I hope you can all sleep at night knowin' that you're celebrating some pussy-ass alligator that doesn't have the sack to face the truth!"

"Suck my dick!" Air Force Gator yelled as he disappeared behind the flag. Barack Obama and Gator's hot stripper girlfriend Trish followed close behind as the president put his hand on the alligator's shoulder.

"Air Force Gator, I'm sorry about what happened out there," the president said. "You should have let the Secret Service take him down."

"I don't need some fucking suits protecting me," Air Force Gator said. "I fight my own fights."

"Regardless, you didn't deserve that. This

is supposed to be a celebration."

"I don't need some ticker tape dog-and-pony show.. I'm honored by you making this holiday, but Trish and I are getting back in the Gator Plane and heading home to New Orleans. It's been an honor and a privilege to serve this great nation, Mr. President."

Air Force Gator offered a salute, which was quickly returned by the president. Lifting his hot stripper girlfriend into his scaly arms, the alligator walked away from the memorial, the president, and his military career.

Chapter III

March 25, 2013

New Orleans, Louisiana

Dirt and leaves swirled through the air of the New Orleans backyard as the Gator Plane lowered into Air Force Gator's backyard. As the giant mouth of the plane's alligator head opened, an exhausted Air Force Gator and his hot stripper girlfriend Trish hopped out. Throwing a tarp over the plane, the alligator let out a sigh.

"You ok, baby?" Trish asked. "You didn't say a word that whole flight."

"That guy was a dickhead, but I'm not gonna let it get me down," Air Force Gator responded. "I've got you, baby, and that's the only thing that matters to me right now and for the rest of my life. Now let's go get drunk, go to town on some boneless wings, watch *Commando* again, and fuck."

"I love you, baby."

"Love you too, hun."

Air Force Gator scooped Trish into his gigantic arms and carried her into his house. Once they were inside, the evil pig farmer Van Buren released his clutch from the underside of the Gator Plane and scurried into a nearby bush. He collapsed to the ground and attempted to massage his aching fingers, sore after hanging on to the exterior of an airplane for over 1,000 miles. Once feeling had returned to his hands, the pig farmer sent a group text message to the rest of the Sons of Gustav.

"*Thirty minutes,*" it read.

Unaware of the presence of the man that crashed the Air Force Gator Day celebration, the alligator and the stripper prepared for a relaxing night.

"Grab that bottle of Old Crow," Air Force Gator said as he collapsed onto the couch. "We're killing that right now."

Trish grabbed the bottle of whiskey and walked towards the military hero.

"Open up," she said.

"Just the way I like it," responded the alligator. He lifted his head towards the ceiling and opened his mouth, exposing over 80 sharp teeth. Trish poured close to a liter of bourbon whiskey into his mouth, stopping shy of emptying the whole bottle.

"What gives?" Air Force Gator said as he belched and wiped his chin. "There's at least five more shots left in there."

"Don't get greedy, baby," Trish said. "I gotta get fucked up, too."

Like her alligator boyfriend, she turned her head skyward and poured the remainder of the bottle down her throat.

"That's my girl," Air Force Gator said, smiling. "Now let me see that sexy tat."

His hot stripper girlfriend smiled as she turned around, teasing the removal of her tank top. Slowly, she raised the bottom of the fabric to reveal her "Gator Bait" tramp stamp.

"That's the ticket, babe," Air Force Gator said, quickly forgetting about the unpleasantness that occurred earlier in Washington. "Actually, hold that thought and go grab us some more booze. I'll put the *Commando* DVD in."

"It's always in the DVD player. You know that. Just sit back and relax, and I'll grab some beers."

Lying back on the couch, Air Force Gator closed his eyes. His moment of relaxation was short lived, as the sudden sounds of screaming, gunfire, and explosions erupted from outside his front door. He sprang to his feet and ran towards the sounds. Throwing the door open, he was greeted by a catastrophic sight. Flames bellowed from the windows of each and every home on the opposite side of his suburban street. As his jaw dropped, his gaze turned upward. A mile in the distance, he saw the skyline of New Orleans. Most of the buildings were ablaze, but several were missing. As he stared at the smoke rising into the sky, he witnessed the Sheraton skyscraper crumble to the ground in a cloud of dust and debris.

"My god..." the alligator muttered as he surveyed the carnage.

His attention was drawn away from the skyline by more local events, as he spotted a car filled with reptiles rolling slowly down the street. The driver was the scarred alligator Pierce, and two sunglasses-wearing crocodiles named Taft and Polk leaned out of the back windows with flamethrowers. A croc named Coolidge stood out of the sunroof, tossing Molotov cocktails at any building that wasn't currently ablaze. Air Force Gator watched flames belch twenty feet out of either side of the car, but none of the four reptiles seemed to have spotted him yet. Ducking behind a bush, the heroic alligator prepared himself for combat. He didn't have time to formulate any real plan, but his instincts told him to act quickly before his neighborhood was nothing but ashes.

As the Molotov-throwing Coolidge turned towards Air Force Gator's house, the hero could only think of Trish. She was blissfully unaware of the horror occurring outside, and Gator didn't want her to learn about it from a sudden smoke alarm. From the sunroof, Coolidge hurled a flaming cocktail towards Air Force Gator's home.

With one giant, GatorAid-enhanced leap, Air Force Gator launched himself through the air, grabbed the Molotov cocktail, and tackled the crocodile out of the sunroof and onto the street. Before the other Sons of Gustav could react, Air Force Gator forcefully rammed the entire Molotov cocktail into the anal cavity of Coolidge. Picking the crocodile up, he then delivered a swift kick to his backside. The glass of the bottle shattered inside of the crocodile, and flames spread throughout his rectum. With his butt completely filled with fire, Coolidge shrieked and comically fled down the street in search of a lake to jump into.

One villainous reptile was disposed of, but the driver and flamethrower crocs were now well aware of Gator's presence. Polk and Taft exited the car as the hero grabbed a nearby mailbox and ripped the post out of the ground. Polk aimed his weapon at Air Force Gator, but didn't have time to pull the trigger. With a golf swing that would make Tiger Woods proud, Gator drove the top of the mailbox directly into the crocodile's testicles. A girlish yelp exited his mouth as he fell to the ground, his testicles ruptured inside of him.

Raising his flamethrower,Taft unleashed a torrent of fire in Air Force Gator's direction. Sidestepping the flames, the hero whipped his GatorAid-enhanced tail towards the weapon. Wrapping around the flamethrower, he attempted to yank it into his own arms. It could only go so far, as the hose was still connected to Taft's back-mounted propane tank.

As the two reptiles tussled over the weapon, Air Force Gator offered a swift headbutt to Taft, staggering him. With the crocodile stunned, Gator sunk his teeth into his shoulder and separated his arm from his torso. Taft opened his jaws wide with a scream as the American hero shoved the nozzle of the flamethrower into his esophagus. He squeezed his claw on the trigger as white-hot flames travelled down Taft's throat and spread throughout his innards. Within a matter of seconds, all of the crocodile's internal organs had been melted into a bubbling goo. Taft's lifeless body fell into a heap on the pavement.

Hearing the sound of pained moans, Air Force Gator turned to see Polk writhing on the street and holding his crushed genitals. He slowly walked towards the injured crocodile, whose eyes grew wide with terror. Polk's moaning turned to pleading as the massive alligator towered above him.

"No, please..." begged the crocodile.

"Please what?"

"Please don't kill me, Air Force Gator. My balls hurt so bad. I promise I'll leave the Sons. I'll never hurt a soul."

"Fuck that," the hero said. "You dickweeds probably scared the shit out of my hot stripper girlfriend by now. I was gonna get laid tonight, but you and your buddies probably fucked that up real good."

As much as Polk's balls hurt, he made a last ditch attempt to dive into the waiting car. He dove headfirst into the back seat, but Air Force Gator grabbed him by the hind claws and began to pull. Polk's front claws dug into the back seat as he struggled to escape. Gator yanked him out without issue and stood him up. A forceful punt to Polk's already-demolished testicles doubled him over, and the hero alligator lifted him up over eight feet in the air. A thundering powerbomb drove the crocodile's body through the roof of the car.

Glancing in his rear view mirror, the driver Pierce watched Gator's combat prowess in awe. The two made brief eye contact with each other, and the scarred driver sensed one last chance to escape with his life. Polk's limp and bloody body was still buried in the steel of the car's roof as Pierce rammed the gas with his claw and sped away.

Standing over Taft's smoldering corpse, Air Force Gator had another chance to survey the damage to the city he called home. The Sons of Gustav had limited numbers, but they had managed to cause an untold amount of damage to New Orleans. Buildings that once reached high above the city's skyline now lie in heaps of smoking rubble. Gator watched the smoke rise into the sky, and his mind immediately returned to that Tuesday morning in 2001 that inspired him to return to his military calling. His claws balled into fists as he began to regret the retirement announcement he had made earlier that day in Washington.

His blood boiled, but his focus was broken by a voice coming from behind him.

"Gator, baby!" Trish yelled from the doorway of the house.

"Trish, get those titties back inside!"

Gator stared at his hot stripper girlfriend as he heard the unmistakable sound of thrusters emanating from his backyard. Leaves scattered around the lawn as the Gator Plane made itself visible. It rose above the house and slowly hovered closer to Air Force Gator. Inside was the same man that had interrupted the ceremony in Washington.

"How ya doin', Gatah?" Van Buren said via the Gator Plane's intercom system.

"Gator baby, who's that man in your plane?" Trish yelled.

"Don't worry about him, honey," Air Force Gator said. "He's just some asshole with a tiny dick. Get back inside."

"You don't know shit about my dick, Gatah!" Van Buren yelled. "My dick is just fine!"

Air Force Gator chuckled and made a "tiny dick" gesture with his claw.

"Fuck you, alligator!" Van Buren said. "You have no idea what I'm capable of. Me and the reptiles you abandoned are gonna bring a reckonin' to this country that's it's deserved for a long time."

"Shut the fuck up and get out of my plane," Air Force Gator said.

"Fat chance. Goodbye, Air Force Gator!"

Van Buren turned the Gator Plane to face the house. With the pull of a trigger, the pig farmer launched a three-missile Trident strike directly at Air Force Gator's house. The roof came down on Trish, burying her in wood and flames.

"No!" Air Force Gator screamed as he sprinted towards the flaming pile of rubble that used to be his home.

With a laugh, Van Buren activated the thrusters of the Gator Plane and soared away, disappearing over the southern horizon.

"Trish, where are you?" Gator asked as he threw flaming pieces of wood aside. He dug through several feet of rubble before finding her body. Her eyes were closed, and her forehead was covered in blood.

"Trish baby, wake up," Gator pleaded as he gently shook her limp body. "I'm here, baby. That dickhead is gone."

No matter how much he pleaded with her or shook her, she didn't react. Gator had seen enough dead bodies in his time to recognize a lost cause, and gently set her down on the lawn. It had been decades since he last cried, but he sobbed quietly as he slowly laid his claw over her face and shut her eyelids.

With tears running down his scaly face, Air Force Gator looked to the sky.

"I'm coming for you, Van Buren. If it's the last thing I do, I'm going to kill the shit out of you and all of your goober friends."

Gator raised his claws into the sky, balled into fists.

"*You hear me, Van Buren?! I'm coming for you!*"

Chapter IV

March 28, 2013

Auyantepui Mountain, Venezuela

Deep in the Venezuelan jungle, a massive plateau towered above the trees below. Above the Angel Falls waterfall that stretched almost a mile into the sky, acres of land had sat completely undisturbed for centuries. That peace had been disturbed for three days now, as a group of dozens of reptiles descended on it via helicopter. After the sacking of New Orleans, the Sons of Gustav enacted the second phase of their evil plot.

Van Buren walked amongst his minions as they set up makeshift barracks, laboratories, and shooting ranges. In the center of the Sons' new operating base sat the Gator Plane. After stealing it and using it to kill Air Force Gator's hot stripper girlfriend, the pig farmer wanted to make it as visible as possible to his followers as a trophy of their successful first phase. Air Force Gator was emotionally crushed, and New Orleans was virtually burnt to the ground. Homes were destroyed by Molotov cocktails, skyscrapers were taken down with well-placed bombs, and reptiles ran through the French Quarter firing assault rifles at anything on two legs. In a final strike before the migration to Venezuela, Van Buren used the Gator Plane to carpet bomb anything still standing in the New Orleans skyline.

They had made headlines across the world with their attack, but the Sons viewed the theft of the Gator Plane as their greatest accomplishment. All of their makeshift buildings were being constructed in a circle around the legendary aircraft, which sat at the center like a holy artifact.

As the pig farmer walked through the Sons' new base, the scarred alligator Pierce stayed by his side. In the months since Van Buren's arrival in New Orleans, Pierce had consistently proven himself as the most cunning and dangerous reptile in the group. Taking on a role as Van Buren's personal adviser and bodyguard, he was the only reptile to receive extensive details on the overall direction of the Sons.

"Bring me our resident egghead," Van Buren said to Pierce as the duo stood in front of the Gator Plane.

A crocodile named Buchanan had exhibited an exceptional mind for engineering, and Van Buren dubbed him the head of research for the Sons of Gustav. His eyesight and passive nature didn't lend themselves to combat, but the pig farmer hoped his intellectual capability would prove to be an asset for the group.

Pierce disappeared for a moment and returned with the scientist.

"You called for me, Mr. Van Buren?" Buchanan asked.

"Sure did, Bucky," Van Buren said,

utilizing a nickname that the crocodile hated. "Take a look at what we got here in front of us. Now tell me, what makes this goddamn plane so hard to swat out of the sky?"

"It would be impossible to say for sure without running tests," Buchanan replied. "But its exterior appears to be abnormally durable. Based on reports from the Crocodile Rock incident and the plane's history with Air Force Gator's grandfather, it's been rumored to be virtually impervious to missile strikes."

"Perfect," Van Buren said. "Bucky, I want this scale armor reverse engineered down to its core. I want it available for our vehicles within two months."

"That may be a tall order, Mr. Van Buren. I've done substantial research into this aircraft, and its armor has puzzled the military's top minds for decades. Air Force Gator's grandfather is the only one who knows for sure how it was constructed, and he's been deceased for quite some time."

"You heard what the boss wants," Pierce said sternly. "Now do it, because I don't want to throw you off that waterfall two months from now."

"My man Pierce here isn't lying," Van Buren said. "Get to work, Bucky."

Nervously, the engineer retreated to the construction that would soon be his laboratory. Grabbing a metal case, he approached the fabled Gator Plane to begin his tests. Van Buren and Pierce nodded in approval as they continued their tour of the base.

Many details of the Sons' operations were revealed to Pierce, but the alligator was still unsure of Van Buren's final objective. After spending some time checking in on the status of the new base's constructions, the duo retreated to the pig farmer's private command room. There, Pierce hoped to have his lingering questions answered.

"Boss, you know I've been by your side every step of the way," Pierce said. "And I'll continue to do so. But if you trust me the way you say you do, I'd love to hear more about what this is all about."

"You've been my most reliable soldier," Van Buren said. "I got no doubt in my mind that you're the best the Sons has to offer, and that's why you're my right hand alligator. But you gotta trust that I know what's best here. Rest assured, we gonna get justice for what that Gator Plane-flyin' son of a bitch did to Papa Gustav."

"But how? You already killed his hot girlfriend and burned his city to the ground. Where do we go from here?"

"That was just phase one, Pierce. We damaged that gator to his core, but we ain't done with him by a long shot. Those stripper titties are dead and gone, and we gonna run that son of a bitch through the ringer more than he ever imagined possible. I could have killed him with his own fuckin' plane."

"Why didn't you?" Pierce asked.

"All part of the plan. Tell me, Pierce my

boy...did you notice that this base is down one reptile?"

"Yeah, Monroe isn't here."

"That's right. That little turtle fella is my man back in the homeland. Thing is, he doesn't even know why he's back there. He doesn't know what his real mission is, but he's gonna carry it out perfectly without even realizing it."

"What's that?"

"That turtle boy was always a little weak, and I don't know what we could have used him for. He's the perfect candidate to make the ultimate sacrifice. Air Force Gator's gonna find him, and he's gonna put that shelled bastard through hell trying to find out where we are. That weak little turtle is gonna give up our location, and that traitor alligator son of a bitch will find his way here, Gator Plane or not."

"Why the hell would we want him here?" Pierce asked. "Surely you know how many plots he's foiled. How many terrorists he's killed..."

"Pierce, we want him here because we've got plans for him. That stupid fuck doesn't have any idea about the hell he's about to walk into."

Chapter V

April 4, 2013

New Orleans, Louisiana

What used to be New Orleans was now little more than rubble. Over a week after the Sons of Gustav launched their attack, most survivors had evacuated the city's remains and relocated to temporary housing elsewhere in the state and country. With Trish dead, Air Force Gator had spent the time in a daze. He survived on the meat of the crocodiles he killed, but found it impossible to feel anything but grief. Clearing the rubble of his former home, he buried the hot stripper and marked her position with the tattered American flag that had been blown off his front porch.

1,500 miles away, Ray "Razor" Connolly could think of nothing but his best friend when he heard the fate of New Orleans. Gator was always good at answering texts in quick fashion, even if they were frequently illegible because of his unwieldy alligator claws. This time, Razor couldn't find any evidence whatsoever that his former partner was even alive.

Booking a flight from Boston to the remains of New Orleans, Razor assumed ownership of an abandoned station wagon and scoured the blood-stained streets for any signs of reptile life. Heading down one suburban avenue, he slammed on the brakes upon spotting a long, scaly tail in the middle of the pavement.

Razor's hand covered his mouth as he cautiously walked towards the reptilian corpse. Fearing the worst, he mentally prepared himself for the vision of his best friend lying in a pool of his own blood. Approaching the body, he quickly discovered that something didn't match up. Discerning between crocodiles and alligators wasn't Razor's strongest suit, but he knew enough to know it wasn't his former partner. Instead, it was the corpse of Polk, still grasping what remained of his testicles as a dented mailbox lay next to him.

Razor's initial moment of relief was immediately interrupted by a voice from behind.

"What the fuck are you doing here, Razor?"

Startled, Razor whipped around and drew the pistol from his waistband. As he readied to defend himself, Razor immediately recognized the scaly face in his crosshairs. With bloodshot eyes and tattered clothes, Air Force Gator had clearly been through hell.

"Gator!" Razor yelled as he dropped his gun. He rushed forward and hugged his distraught alligator friend. "I thought you were dead, buddy. You've gotta answer those texts...I was scared to death."

Air Force Gator didn't respond verbally, but Razor could sense his friend's fragile mental state by feeling the alligator's body shake as he sobbed.

"Buddy, I don't know what to say. Who did this?"

After returning to his Boston bartending gig following the events of Crocodile Rock, Razor had done his best to avoid the news. He was proud of playing a part in taking Gustav down, but the death of Colonel Backlund had made him want to stay as far from combat as possible. Air Force Gator may have continued to fly sorties for those eight years, but Razor couldn't bring himself to get back into action.

"You know what, it doesn't matter," Razor said as he patted the back of his shattered best friend. "I read about what happened down here. Sounds like a lot of people are heading about sixty miles southwest to Houma. Let's grab a hotel or something and get you right again."

"Fuck the hotel," Gator said through tears as he broke his silence. "Take me to a bar down there. We're getting fucked up."

Despite Air Force Gator keeping his alcohol intake under control for over a decade, his friend knew that he'd have to tread lightly given the circumstances. It was Grandpa Gator's death that triggered Air Force Gator's first slide into uncontrollable alcoholism, and Razor knew that he must be similarly devastated considering how super hot Trish was.

"Deal. We'll have some drinks, but let's focus on getting your head right tomorrow."

For over an hour, Razor and Gator sat in the station wagon in silence. Gator rested his snout on the window and wordlessly stared out into the evening sky, fogging the window as he cried with occasional gross alligator snorts.

Pulling the station wagon into the parking lot of Jimmy C's Tavern in Houma, Razor attempted to cheer up his alligator friend.

"Whole lotta booze in there, buddy," Razor said. "And plenty of time before last call. Let's get some liquid therapy into you tonight, and we'll get your head right tomorrow. First round's on me."

They entered the shady tavern, saddled up at the bar, and ordered shots. Before Razor could even toast his friend, the Jim Beam was already heaved back into the alligator's throat.

"Six more of those," Air Force Gator said.

With a chuckle, the bartender poured half a dozen shots of Beam and slid them across the counter towards the alligator. Grasping the glasses with his claws, Gator simultaneously took all six shots.

"Let's pump the breaks a little bit, buddy," Razor said. "We've got plenty to talk about, and you're on a fast track towards incoherent. Pace yourself, we've got all night."

"I know you're trying to help," Air Force Gator said as he wiped whiskey dribble off of his jaw. "But I'm not in the mood tonight to deal with anything. I just need to get fucked up and get laid. Can you let me do that?"

Razor had seen Gator like this before, and knew that there was no talking him down. Knowing that the alligator would be belligerent and most likely kicked out of the bar by night's end, Razor stopped drinking.

As Razor babysat his friend, he briefly made eye contact with a curious figure at a table in the corner of the bar. There, a turtle sat. When Razor met eyes with him, the tiny green figure quickly looked away. Razor was only vaguely familiar with the Sons of Gustav, and he didn't recognize that he had just laid eyes on the group's sole turtle and only member still in the United States.

Monroe was nervous about being spotted, but assumed he was safe as long as Air Force Gator wasn't aware of his presence. Retreating his head halfway into his shell, the turtle began compulsively scratching at the label of his beer with his tiny claws. Van Buren had trusted him to be the Sons' eyes and ears back in the states, and Monroe was going to fulfill his duties by keeping tabs on their biggest threat. Luckily for him, the Sons' biggest threat was on a fast track to blacking out at the bar.

Fifteen shots deep, Air Force Gator ungracefully attempted to stand up out of his stool. He stumbled a bit on his way to the bathroom and leaned against the bar for support. Glancing next to him with glazed-over eyes, he spotted an attractive blonde.

"HEY, YOU EVER FUCK AN ALLIGATOR?" Air Force Gator slurred way too loudly into her ear.

Leaning back in disgust, the woman grabbed the arm of the large man next to her.

"Chris, this drunk-ass alligator is trying to fuck me!" she said as her boyfriend quickly stood up and approached the intoxicated American hero.

Grabbing Air Force Gator by the collar of his trademark bomber jacket, the boyfriend clearly didn't appreciate the war hero's drunken advances on his girl.

"Listen up you reptile son of a bitch," Chris said. "You've got a lot of nerve showing up here after your kind took out New Orleans."

"I'm not...I'm not one of them," Air Force Gator mumbled.

Glancing at the top of Gator's head, he noticed the trademark goggles of a legend.

"Wait a second..." Chris said. "You're right. You're...you're Air Force Gator, aren't you? Yeah, yeah, I recognize you for sure. I saw you on the news flexing like an idiot in Washington about a week back. Last I heard, you let your chick die when they attacked New Orleans. You couldn't keep your girl alive and now you show up here and try to pick mine up? Get the fuck out here, loser."

Gator had tried to shove the memories of Trish into the back of his mind all night, but the combination of his current intoxication and the harsh words of Chris sent him into a rage.

Before the blonde's boyfriend could react, Air Force Gator pulled a switchblade from his pocket, whipped it open with the flick of his wrist, and plunged it directly into Chris's right eye. He fell to the ground screaming, blood spraying out of the wounded socket. Raising his massive foot over the man's head, the alligator prepared a deadly stomp.

With the swing of a pool cue, another patron interrupted what would have certainly become a murder. The wood cracked across Air Force Gator's temple, and it was just enough to refocus his rage on a new target. Lowering his shoulder, the alligator charged the man and drove him directly through the bar's wall into the parking lot. Covered in dust and wood splinters, Gator grabbed a large rock and raised it into the air. He snarled and prepared to strike, but a boot made contact with the rock before he could bring it down. As the rock flew through the air, Gator looked up to see his friend.

"Gator, what the fuck is the matter with you?" Razor asked. "We gotta split right now."

Razor helped his drunken friend stand and quickly escorted him to the passenger seat of his station wagon. With the rest of the bar patrons yelling at the two and the sounds of an ambulance roaring down the street in the distance, the two friends took off down the road. Two miles west of the bar, Razor pulled the car over.

"The fuck, Gator?" Razor said. "I take you out to get your head right, and you almost killed two guys."

"They were fucking with me."

"No they weren't, man. One guy was defending his girl and the other didn't want to see a man die at the bar. You realize you're this close to being guilty of murder, right?"

"I wasn't gonna kill that guy in the parking lot," Gator said. "I was gonna hit him with a rock until he passed out and then I was gonna pee on him."

"Either way, you put a damn knife in that dude's eye. Good thing that ambulance was showing up when you left, because he could have died."

Gator hung his head down and sighed. In the middle of the night, the two friends sat in silence for several minutes.

"This isn't you, Gator," Razor said. "This isn't the alligator that just had a national holiday enacted in his name. This isn't the gator that killed Osama bin Laden. This isn't the gator that stopped Gustav from killing millions of people, and this certainly isn't the gator that I consider my friend."

With tears welling in his eyes, the alligator looked up at his former partner.

"Where would I even start?" Gator asked. "He took my Gator Plane. What would Grandpa Gator think if he knew?"

"He'd wonder when his grandson turned into some sad-sack pussy. This is not you. You don't give up in hard times. You've risen from tragedy before, and you can do it again. You're not the alligator who gets down on himself and gives up, you're the alligator that brings it to those sons of bitches."

Wiping the tears from his eyes, Air Force Gator felt suddenly sober despite the staggering amount of alcohol running through his system.

"But where do we even start?" Gator asked.

At that moment, a van drove past the sign that Gator and Razor were parked behind. In the driver's seat was Monroe.

"You see that turtle?" Razor smiled. "He was giving us a look all night like he was up to something. Seemed like he had it out for you."

"Not all reptiles are in the Sons. That's not a lead."

"I may not know much about these Sons," Razor said. "But I got a good look at the guy as I was heading to the pisser. Had an emblem on his little turtle jacket that had the silhouette of a crocodile holding a bolt of lightning in his fist. That mean anything to you?"

Air Force Gator perked up.

"That's their goddamn crest. Razor, put your foot on the fucking pedal and follow that van."

Without a moment of hesitation, Razor whipped the station wagon around and began pursuing the white van. Air Force Gator splashed a bottle of water in his face and slapped his own cheeks, attempting to sober his mind as much as possible for the current situation.

After several miles, the two saw the red brake lights of the van light up on what appeared to be an unpopulated rural road.

"Stop the car," Air Force Gator told Razor. "Kill the lights."

Razor pulled over into the grass, turned

off his headlights, and shut down the engine to make sure the turtle couldn't detect their presence. Staring down the road, the duo could tell that Monroe had pulled into the driveway of a residence of some sort. It was far too dark on this country road to make out any specific structures, but they heard the car door open and close as the turtle exited.

"This has gotta be his home," Razor said. "Wanna wait for him to fall asleep and then get the jump on him?"

"Why the fuck does a turtle need a house?" Air Force Gator asked. "Fuck it. Doesn't matter. Also doesn't matter if I go in there when he's sleeping, shitting, eating, or anything else. He's a fucking turtle...do you really think I'm gonna have trouble beating the shit out of him?"

"Probably not," Razor said. "But you're wasted, and he could be armed. You just play it safe if you're going in there. I'll stay out here in the weeds and grab him if he tries to run. That turtle is bound to bolt as soon as he knows you're on to him."

"That little dickhead isn't gonna hear shit until it's way too late," Air Force Gator said as he pulled a flask of Old Crow out of his bomber jacket. Forgetting his prior attempt to sober his mind, he took a long swig, placed it back in his pocket, and exited the station wagon.

Razor stayed behind as Air Force Gator silently crawled through the thick weeds on his belly. As he approached his destination, it became clear that the structure in question was indeed a swamp house. Sneaking around the back, he discovered a patio door that was locked with a variety of bolts and padlocks. Upon circling around to the front of the house, he discovered the same for that entrance. With the spontaneity of this operation, Gator wasn't equipped with an earpiece or radio to speak to Razor with. He'd have to find another way in by himself.

He spent a moment considering crawling in through an unlocked window, but the solution was right in front of him on the door itself. A doggie door sat at the bottom, and a slight nudge with his foot revealed to Air Force Gator that it wasn't secured.

At eight feet tall with bulging, GatorAid-infused muscles, Air Force Gator didn't expect an easy entry. Crouching down, he discovered that his elongated head squeezed through with ease. His shoulders and torso were a different story. Twisting and turning, the alligator attempted to find an angle that would allow his entire body into the house. He struggled for a moment or two before stopping to listen to his surroundings.

Everything was dark inside the house, and it was completely silent outside of a slight mechanical whirring. Gator listened for a moment, and quickly realized it was the sound of a turtle using a motorized toothbrush in an upstairs bathroom. With such a tiny little turtle head, even the sound of a toothbrush rattling around his skull was bound to be enough to mask sounds coming from downstairs.

"Fuck it," Air Force Gator said as he flexed his muscles and shattered the door around him. He stood upright in the kitchen as the splinters of the door fell to the tile floor.

Following the noise, the alligator made his way through the darkened kitchen and living room as he looked for stairs. He ran his claw softly against the walls as he crept forward, eventually finding the way up. Taking each step slower than the last, he heard the sound of the toothbrush grow louder as the light from the bathroom became visible.

Air Force Gator rounded one last corner into the bedroom, and the profile of Monroe became visible through the bathroom door. Wearing pajamas, the tiny turtle was standing on a large stool as he brushed his teeth in the mirror. He gargled with water, spit into the sink, and then reached for his contact lens case. Gator recognized that it was the perfect time to strike. As the turtle tilted his head up and began to take his first contact out, the alligator sprung into action and kicked the footstool out from under him. With a crash, the pajama-clad turtle fell to the ground below.

Grabbing the startled turtle with one claw, Air Force Gator began flicking at his tiny little head with the other.

"How do you like that, you god damn turtle?" Gator asked as he repeatedly flicked Monroe's head.

"Ow! Ow! Ow!" the turtle yelped, retreating back into his shell to avoid further flicks.

"Where is he? Where is that limpdick redneck?"

"You won't get a single solitary word from me, you traitor!" Monroe said from inside the shell.

With a mighty toss, Air Force Gator sent Monroe's shell crashing into the mirror. Glass shattered around the bathroom as the alligator picked up the turtle once again.

"Ha!" Monroe laughed. "You think I felt any of that?"

"Probably not," Air Force Gator responded. "But you'll sure as fuck feel it when I jam a piece of this mirror up your stupid little turtle butthole."

The alligator grabbed a large shard of broken glass and tapped it against the turtle's shell.

"No no...not that!"

"I'll count down from three..."

Before Air Force Gator could even begin counting, Monroe cracked.

"Alright, fine!" Monroe said. "He said he's going down to South America to set up shop on top of the world's biggest waterfall. Angel...Angel Falls, I think is the name."

"What's his plan?" Gator asked. "Why does he need my plane? What's he putting together down in South America? What's he doing on top of some dumbass waterfall?"

"He said something about 'making an example of Air Force Gator.' I don't know anything else. I swear I don't."

"How about now?"

Air Force Gator gripped the turtle tight and began rubbing the shell against his ass.

"Noooo!" Monroe yelled as his pajamas and shell slid against the alligator's rear. "This is super gross! Please stop!"

Gator stopped and raised the turtle up again so they could see each other face to face.

"I am not fucking with you here," Air Force Gator said. "Tell me what he's doing down there, or you're fucking dead."

"I swear I don't know! Van Buren just told me to stay here in the States and keep an eye on you. He'll kill me if he finds out that I told you anything."

"Well he can thank me for scratching one item off his to-do list."

With another throw, Air Force Gator sent the turtle flying out of the second story window and crashing to the ground below. Across the lawn, Razor heard the sound of shattering glass and raised his head above the weeds to see what caused it. He saw a turtle in tattered, soiled pajamas standing up and dusting himself off. When the turtle began sprinting towards the road, Razor sprung into action.

High-stepping through the tall weeds surrounding Monroe's house, Razor wasn't about to let the turtle make a successful break for it. After a full sprint, he reared his leg up and punted the turtle through the air. Monroe yelled as his shell slammed against the side of his house and his body fell to the lawn once again.

Exiting the house via the front door, Air Force Gator saw Monroe grimacing on the ground. The turtle attempted to hold his injured back, but his tiny little turtle arms couldn't reach around far enough. Picking him up with his claw, the alligator stared directly into Monroe's eyes.

"You have one more chance to tell me what he's planning," Gator said. "One more chance before I kill the shit out of you, you pussy-ass turtle."

"You'll never stop Van Buren," the turtle responded. "I meant it when I said I didn't know anything about his next move, but I know full well what he's capable of. He'll pull it off, and thousands more Americans will die. Burn in hell, Air Force Gator."

Gritting his teeth, Air Force Gator turned towards the road and tossed Monroe one last time. As the turtle soared through the air, an 18-wheeler approached at 70 miles per hour. Its sleepy driver didn't have time to hit the brakes, and he didn't see the screaming reptile heading directly towards his grill. Monroe's body met the semi truck, and the sound of his shell shattering echoed across the Louisiana night. Turtle flesh and shell particles exploded in every direction like shrapnel from a grenade.

"Fuck, man," Razor said as he wiped cold blood from his face. "You killed the shit out of that turtle."

"He's not the last reptile that I'm gonna kill," Air Force Gator said. "Not by a long shot."

"That's the Air Force Gator I know."

"You know all that shit I said in Washington about retiring? I wasn't lying. All I wanted to do was lay around the rest of my life and get drunk and bang that hot stripper. Then this Van Buren motherfucker wrangled up a bunch of crocs, burned my town, stole my plane, and shot a missile at Trish's pretty face. Maybe I really will retire soon, but not before I get down to South America and kill the fucking shit out of that redneck son of a bitch. Now let's go get some big-ass guns."

Chapter VI

April 5, 2013

Houma, Louisiana

Pulling their beat-up station wagon into the parking lot of Jarrett's Military Surplus in Houma, Air Force Gator and Razor scanned the area for security cameras and possible onlookers. At 3:30 in the morning on a weekend, it was unlikely for anyone in this small town to be awake or sober enough to care about or notice what this alligator and bartender were planning.

"I think we should be good," Air Force Gator said as he exited the car. "Let's get in and out as quickly as we can. I wanna be down in South America within 48 hours."

"No need to be hasty," Razor said. "You know I like to err on the side of caution, so I called up a buddy that has our back if shit goes down tonight. Last I heard, he landed about 30 minutes ago."

"You had someone *fly in* to give us backup?"

Just as those words left Air Force Gator's mouth, an unassuming Lincoln Continental pulled into the lot. Its engine turned off and the door opened. A man with dark features and a mustache stepped out of the car, sunglasses obscuring his eyes. With a confident stride, he walked over and shook the hands of Gator and Razor.

"Razor, it's been a while," the man said. "Glad to see you again. And Gator, it hasn't been quite as long since you and I last met."

"Am I missing something here?" Gator said as he turned to Razor. "Who the fuck is this dude?"

"This is my good friend Barry," Razor said with a smirk.

Barry took his sunglasses off and peeled back what was revealed as a fake mustache, raising his finger to his lips in an effort to keep his identity a secret. It was President Barack Obama.

Air Force Gator smiled.

"Ohhh, Barry. That's right. Sorry I didn't recognize you with the new mustache."

"Listen, Gator," Obama said. "Razor told me about what you guys learned from that turtle. Not to mention, I heard on the news about what happened to your girlfriend. It really is a shame, Gator. She was really hot."

"Yeah..." Gator said as he looked down at the ground and kicked a rock across the parking lot. "She really was."

"That's why I'm here to help you guys. Even though I'm the president, it would take too long to get the green light for an official strike on Angel Falls. I know Van Buren is there, and you do too. More importantly, you've got more reason than anyone to want him dead."

"You're god damn right, Mr. President," Gator said before realizing his mistake. "Sorry, I mean Barry."

"I can't get you access to any official U.S. military weaponry, but I want to help you get your claws on anything that you can use against that redneck and his crocs. If the cops show up tonight, I'll pull the president card and get you out of it."

"Good to know," Gator said. "We can use all the help we can get."

"That's not all I've got for you," Obama said as he popped the trunk of his Continental. "I had planned on presenting this to you at the end of the Air Force Gator Day celebration. That is, until Van Buren decided to crash the party. It's custom-made for you, developed by America's top military engineers. It's too heavy for me to pull out of the trunk, but you shouldn't have any problem."

Air Force Gator walked over to the trunk and looked inside. There sat a massive minigun that featured a spinning barrel that jutted out of an actual crocodile head.

"Say hello to the Croc Blocker," President Obama said. "Two hundred pounds of reptile-killing power. A four-foot barrel that cranks out 8,000 rounds per minute. This weapon can take down a crocodile, an airplane, or a god damn battleship."

"This is incredible," Air Force Gator said as he lovingly held his new favorite toy. "You obviously know that I love theatrics, considering the barrel is coming out of a fucking crocodile head."

"Not just any crocodile head, Air Force Gator. When the Coast Guard was running cleanup on Crocodile Rock all those years ago, they made a discovery. You launched Gustav sky high and blew him to bits, but part of him separated with the initial grenade explosion and washed up onshore. For years, military scientists kept his head in storage in the hopes of studying such an advanced reptilian brain. I told those nerds that I had a better idea for it. Every time you use the Croc Blocker, you'll be firing bullets straight out of the mouth of your most notable kill."

"*No shit...*" Air Force Gator said as he stared at the head and began to laugh. "Gustav, you old shithead! Remember how you were gonna take America down, but then I flew down to your little fort and killed the fucking shit out of you and all of your idiot buddies? Now your head's on my gun!"

Gator gave Gustav's decapitated head a noogie.

"Oh man, Barry," Gator said as he looked up at the president. "This is just the fucking best. Rest assured, I'm gonna light up plenty of assholes with this piece of work."

"I don't doubt it," Obama said. "But I know you need more than one big-ass gun, and we both want to get you on the road as soon as possible. I grabbed one of the CIA's breaching kits on the way out the door, so I've got all we need to pick this store's lock and disable their security."

"Don't worry about picking the lock," Gator said. "Do whatever you gotta do to disable the alarm, but I can find my own way in."

With that, Air Force Gator offered a swift salute to President Obama, then began digging through the concrete of the parking lot. Razor had seen him do this plenty of times before, but the president was impressed as he saw the speed in which the heroic alligator burrowed through the ground.

As Gator made his way towards the surplus store, he couldn't help but feel a wave of pleasant nostalgia come over him. Surprising Osama bin Laden back in 2005 and tearing the al Qaeda leader's tiny penis off was one of the happiest moments of the alligator's life. His nostalgia quickly turned to determination, as he knew he had to offer a similarly painful death to the villainous pig farmer from Tennessee.

Once he was situated underneath the store, Gator turned up and breached through the floor. With no target to sneak up on, he was less concerned about staying quiet than he had been on the fateful Abbottabad raid that took down bin Laden. No alarms were triggered as he burst through the floor, but he knew it was a matter of time. Running over to the front door, he disengaged the lock and President Obama and Razor entered. As soon as they entered, an alarm began ringing.

"Grab what you need," Obama said. "I've got the alarm."

Air Force Gator grabbed two equipment bags and kicked down the door to the storage room in the back of the store. Row upon row of assault rifles, rocket launchers, and grenades lined the metal racks. He immediately began filling both bags with anything and everything that would fit.

"Good lord, man," Razor said from the storage room doorway. "You gonna use all that?"

"I feel like I'm on *Supermarket Sweep*," Gator said. "And I'm just filling my cart with turkeys."

Gator filled both bags to the brim just as Obama finished shutting the alarm down with the CIA kit. Hearing a sound from elsewhere in the store, the three turned to the source. There, an elderly man in his pajamas stood in a doorway.

"The sam hell's goin' on in here?" the old, bald man said.

He quickly reached under the front counter and grabbed a pistol. Aiming it at Razor, he offered a warning.

"You boys best get out of my store," he said. "This ain't just a store, this is my home. And if you don't drop everything you grabbed right now, you're gonna get an ass full of lead."

Air Force Gator, Razor, and Obama held their hands over their heads and slowly backed towards the door.

"Sir, I'm going to move very slowly," said President Obama. He held a flashlight to his face and slowly removed his fake mustache.

"Mr. President?" the shop owner said.

"That's right," Obama said. "And I need you to trust me. America has an enemy that's preparing to strike, and Air Force Gator is the only one that I trust to save us. He needs what you have in this store. Please, for the love of your country, let us leave and never speak of this."

The old man lowered his gun and let out a slight chuckle.

"You know, the boys at the meetings keep sayin' that you're trying to take our guns." the old man said. "Can't say I ever saw it going down like this."

"I'll double your stock when the country is safe," Obama said. "Rest assured that your weapons will be used to kill some total dicks."

"I may not have voted for you," the old man said. "But I serve the United States first and foremost. And Gator Boy, I gotta say I've always had respect for your service."

Air Force Gator nodded.

"Alright," the old man said. "You boys mosey on outta here. Take what you've got with ya, and keep us hard-working Americans safe."

"I won't forget this," the president said. "You'll receive a personal invite to the White House when Gator's done with his job, and the first beer's on me."

"I'll hold ya to that, chief," the man said.

Gator, Razor, and Obama walked back towards the parking lot. Stuffing the equipment bags into the trunk of the station wagon, the men fully understood the importance of coming events. Within a few days, all three of the men would go their separate ways and an unofficial mission to take out Van Buren would be underway.

"Radio me or Razor if there's anything you need," Obama said. "We're here to have your back."

"I'm not taking a radio," Air Force Gator said. "I'm not letting the President take the fall if I fuck this up, so you need to have plausible deniability. And it's sure as shit not gonna fall on my buddy Razor here."

"You think you can take them down alone?" Razor asked. "They just took down one of the country's major cities with a few dozen reptiles and some hick. They're dangerous."

"The moment they killed that hot stripper of mine is the moment they made this my war. I do this, and I do it alone."

Gator saluted the president and entered the passenger seat of Razor's car. Razor saluted and joined him, and Obama stepped back into his Continental. The president started his trip back to Washington, and the station wagon headed south to the Gulf Coast.

Armed with his new Croc Blocker, two bags full of guns and explosives, and knowing little more than the name of a waterfall, Air Force

Gator was fully prepared to travel to South America to kill the shit out of a pig farmer.

DAN RYCKERT

Chapter VII

April 9, 2013

Auyantepui Mountain, Venezuela

Hoover and Truman had been designated security crocodiles by Van Buren, and they were stationed on the edge of the Angel Falls plateau. Sitting in wooden chairs and smoking cigarettes, the reptiles had little to do during the days outside of playing cards, drinking beers, and wondering what their human leader was planning.

"Is this what you pictured when you joined up with the Sons?" Hoover asked Truman.

It had been over two weeks since the Sons of Gustav first landed on the plateau and begun to set up their operating base. In that time, the only activity the two scouts had seen below was the migration of monkeys and the occasional ship in the distance.

"Not exactly, but every cog on the wheel helps the overall mission. If us looking at treetops all day helps Van Buren plan his attack, then I'm here to do my job."

"But what about that night in the bingo hall? He made it sound like we'd be spending our days ripping heads off and our nights dining on humans. I haven't killed a single human since New Orleans."

During the attack on New Orleans, Hoover distinguished himself by killing more humans than any other member of the Sons. Assigned to Bourbon Street, he ran down the length of the tourist destination with a razor-sharp machete, hacking the heads off of travellers and New Orleans natives alike. Ever since the attack, he had worn a necklace that he fashioned out of his victim's teeth.

Truman was a quiet soldier, more than willing to take on Van Buren's less glamorous assignments. Most of his involvement in the New Orleans attack was relegated to planning which buildings would be bombed and which streets would be raided in the effort to rack up as many civilian casualties as possible.

"These things don't happen overnight," Truman said. "Van Buren and the guys in the lab need time to prepare whatever they're planning. We're here to sound the alarms if we see anyone approaching, so we're crucial to this operation."

"It's just so fucking boring."

Suddenly, they heard footsteps behind them.

"Fucking boring, eh?" a voice said.

Turning around, the guards spotted the scarred alligator Pierce.

"Nothing, sir," Hoover said as he saluted. As the top-ranking reptile and the right hand of Van Buren, Pierce had command over the Sons.

"I got the gist of that little chat," Pierce said. "We could kill a few dozen, maybe a few hundred humans if we strike now. Or, we could kill tens of thousands if we wait and see the plan through."

As much as he wanted immediate gratification, Hoover knew Pierce was right.

"Agreed," Hoover said. "I apologize for my loose tongue and lack of patience."

"Good," Pierce said. "Now what's your report for this afternoon?"

"Not much, as usual," Truman said. "We saw a little raft wash up on shore about an hour ago, but it's probably just one of the locals trying to gather fish for the market."

Pierce stared at the two guards, then looked at the coast. It wasn't like Air Force Gator to arrive by sea, but he may have explored other options ever since losing his Gator Plane.

"Look alive today, boys," Pierce said. "You may be right about it being a local, but it's your ass on the line if you're wrong."

Pierce turned and walked back to the main area of the base, continuing his daily checks of every aspect of Van Buren's operation. Ever the diligent soldier, the alligator worked longer hours than any other member of the Sons. He did this despite his growing frustration that their human leader wouldn't let him in on the full details regarding the attack on America. After years of being the pig farmer's most trusted follower and most intelligent reptile, he couldn't shake the feeling that he could offer more to the effort. He shook the nagging concerns from his mind as he continued to do the rounds, leaving Truman and Hoover at their post.

"Why are we taking orders from an alligator, anyway?" Hoover asked once Pierce was out of earshot. "There's a reason he's the only surviving alligator in the Sons. The rest of those idiots got shot by cops back in New Orleans. I heard that Van Buren hasn't heard any updates from that turtle back home, either. You ask me, us crocs are the only capable reptiles there are."

"Van Buren wants to help all reptiles, not just crocodiles," Truman replied. "We're one family down here. No snake is above any turtle, no gator above any crocodile."

As he finished that statement, a scaly claw reached up from the edge of the plateau and grabbed his ankle.

"You haven't met this gator, asshole."

Before Truman even realized what had happened, Air Force Gator had used his right arm to pull him over the edge. With a mighty swing, Gator swung the crocodile's head into the side of the rocky plateau. Truman's head exploded like a watermelon, and Gator tossed his lifeless body towards the jungle floor almost a mile below.

"The fuck?!" Hoover exclaimed as he witnessed the assault. He hadn't seen the assailant, only Truman's decapitated body as it was thrown off the cliff.

Air Force Gator pulled himself over the edge and stood in front of Hoover, two giant equipment bags strapped to his back. No man or standard alligator could have scaled the steep sides of Angel Falls, but Air Force Gator utilized his extreme GatorAid strength to bound up the side of the plateau.

Hoover panicked and reached down to pick up his gun from the ground. With a single kick, Air Force Gator connected with the underside of the crocodile's jaw and shattered every one of his 68 teeth.

"AGGGGGHHH!" Hoover exclaimed as he stumbled back, holding his claws up to his bloodied mouth.

"What's up, d-bag?" Air Force Gator said as Hoover continued to howl. "Ready for some reptile dysfunction?"

With a tap of the back side of his claw, Air Force Gator struck Hoover's testicles. The crocodile's hands now covering his injured balls, his bloody jaw and throat were exposed. Air Force Gator ripped the tooth necklace off of Hoover and put a single massive claw around his throat. Lifting the crocodile high above his head, Air Force Gator forced his body down over the side of the cliff. Hoover let out gargled screams as he plunged towards the jungle below. His body never even made contact with the floor, as the crocodile's torso landed directly on the top of a tree. He had been falling at great speed, and the tree plunged directly through his torso.A streak of cold, reptilian blood painted over twenty feet of the trunk as the murderous reptile breathed his last breath.

"Poor sap," Air Force Gator said as he grabbed his bags and headed towards Van Buren's camp.

Scampering up a small hill, Gator pulled out his binoculars. He laid on his belly in the dirt and peered through the eyepieces to get his first in-person glimpse of the new headquarters of the Sons of Gustav. In a short amount of time, the pig farmer and his crocodile cohorts had transformed the shacks and makeshift barracks of their initial arrival into a full-scale compound. Armed reptiles patrolled around over a dozen concrete buildings, and a ten-foot razor wire fence surrounded the area. Only one entrance was visible, and it was flanked by watchtowers that housed sniper crocs.

As he scanned the area through his binoculars, he stopped on one familiar sight.

"Motherfuckers..." Air Force Gator said as he saw the Gator Plane at the center of the compound. Two crocodiles sat on top of its wing, eating sandwiches on their lunch break.

Gator gritted his teeth and tried to shake off his anger. He switched to the thermal filter on his binoculars and did another scan of the area. Counting over 25 heat signatures, he knew it wouldn't be easy to destroy the base, kill Van Buren and his men, and escape with his plane. In any other circumstance, he'd have loaded the Gator Plane with enough bombs to level the Kremlin and gone to town on these assholes. The Gator Plane wasn't an option any more, but that wasn't the only reason he wasn't taking to the skies. He wanted to see into the eyes of Van Buren as he choked the life out of him.

Taking the snipers out was Air Force Gator's first priority, but he knew alarms would sound as soon as he shot one of them. He'd have to take both of them out in short time to avoid having his presence known immediately.

Changing position, Gator found a tree that stood perfectly in line with both of the guard towers. Over 500 feet from the sniper crocs, there was little chance they'd be aware of their new visitor. Leaving his bags on the ground, the alligator grabbed a sniper rifle between his teeth and began to climb the tree.

Once he was at the right height, Air Force Gator gingerly crawled out on top of a particularly sturdy branch. Balancing his sniper rifle across his forearm, he peered through the scope. His positioning was on point, as both crocodiles were perfectly lined up. One leaned against the back of his post smoking a cigarette, and the second was in an almost identical position 50 feet past him.

Holding his breath, Air Force Gator softly pulled the trigger of his M-24. A muffled sound escaped the chamber as the bullet began its path. Within half a second, the single bullet had passed straight through the brains of both crocodiles. Dropping to the ground simultaneously, there was little chance anyone in the camp was keen to their newly-reduced population.

Gripping the rifle in his huge jaw once again, Air Force Gator rolled off the branch and landed on all four claws on the ground below. He grabbed his bags and began sneaking toward the base. Snipers no longer guarded the front entrance, but it would still be too obvious of an approach. Instead, he made his way to the back of the compound.

Infiltrating bases by digging beneath them had worked for years for the alligator, and he had no reason to deviate from his go-to plan here in Venezuela. He dug his claws into the soft soil behind the base, and made his way underground.

With two bags of weapons strapped to his back, Gator wasn't able to scurry underground as fast as he usually did. It wound up being a blessing in disguise, as his slower speed tipped him off to Van Buren's underground defenses before it was too late

"Well son of a bitch," Air Force Gator said as he stopped just shy of a circular land mine that lay beneath the perimeter of the compound.

Looking left and right in his tunnel, Gator could tell that it wasn't the only explosive. Van Buren must have done his homework, and knew that Gator would attempt an underground approach. It was likely that the entire area was surrounded with clusters of land mines.

No stranger to changing plans on the fly, Air Force Gator scooted backwards in his tunnel and reached into his equipment bag. He didn't have much room to maneuver, but he was able to fumble through the bag with his claw until he felt the charge for his remotely-detonated C4. Leaving the explosive near the mine, he carefully backed his way out of the hole and emerged in the daylight once again behind the base.

Stealth had to be abandoned thanks to Gator's discovery, but he was always prepared for a full-on assault. Reaching back into his bags, he grabbed two items. One was the detonator for his C4. The other was the Croc Blocker. Gator smirked as he looked at the head of Gustav at the end of the barrel, relishing the idea of mowing down the villainous crocodile's followers with bullets fired straight from their idol's decapitated head.

From his thermal scan of the base, it seemed that the majority of the Sons were inside of buildings or eating lunch at the time. A few soldiers were on patrol, but Gator had already taken care of the two scouts at the edge of the plateau and the two sniper crocs in the tower. If there were ever a time for an explosive entrance, this was it.

Air Force Gator inhaled deeply, then flipped the safety of his detonator. Closing his eyes and soaking in the moment, he depressed the red button with his scaly thumb. A brief moment of silence passed before the carnage began. A giant explosion rose from the ground above the mines Gator encountered, and the razor wire fence collapsed to the ground.

Grabbing his Croc Blocker and preparing to make his grand entrance, Gator stopped when he noticed an unforseen consequence of his breach. His suspicion of a perimeter of mines proved true, as a chain reaction of explosions spread out beyond the initial detonation point. A string of explosions were set off in succession, surrounding the entire base. Mines had been placed underneath the full length of the fence, and each of them was triggered by the destruction of the one before it.

In under fifteen seconds, over 100 mines exploded around the compound. What used to be an impenetrable base surrounded by razor wire was now a wide open playground that begged for Air Force Gator's unopposed approach.

Alarms sounded as the Sons of Gustav grabbed their guns and attempted to discover the source of the breach. They were surrounded by the rubble of the fence and outer buildings, and had no way of discerning which direction their attacker was coming from.

Suddenly, every set of ears in the camp heard the sound of a mechanical whirring coming from the rear of the compound. Through the smoke and debris of the explosions, Air Force Gator appeared with the barrel of the Croc Blocker spinning at frightening speed. When the barrel reached full bore, a torrent of gunfire erupted from the mouth of Gustav.

Before any of the crocodiles could take cover, their bodies began being ripped to shreds one by one thanks to the firepower provided by Obama's gift. Entire crocodile heads exploded like watermelons, and Air Force Gator couldn't help but rear his head back and laugh as the remaining buildings of Van Buren's base sported a new coat of paint consisting of blood and scales.

One crocodile charged Air Force Gator with a machete, but he was spotted in Gator's peripheral vision. Swinging the Croc Blocker around, the alligator used the minigun to separate his attacker's legs from his body. Crawling on the ground with blood pouring from his leg stumps, the crocodile looked up at Air Force Gator.

"You're no reptile," the dying croc said. "You're a demon. You slaughter your own kind without remorse."

"You've got that right, fuckhead."

Aiming the Croc Blocker at the legless reptile, Air Force Gator unloaded several hundred rounds directly into his face. When the barrel stopped spinning, all that was left where the crocodile's head used to be was a jawbone and a pile of teeth.

Taking a moment to survey the damage around him, Gator counted over twenty dead crocodiles in the surrounding dirt. His count was a rough estimate, as most of them had been reduced to a red mist that hung in the air of Van Buren's base. Gator expected more of a resistance, but no other signs of life made themselves apparent as he scanned the bloody scene.

Through the dust and blood, Air Force Gator heard the noise of a bell approaching him.

A small silhouette appeared near the ground as
Gator readied his Croc Blocker for whatever it
may be. His finger loosened on the trigger as he
saw what was causing the noise.

A single pig walked through the smoke, a
bell hanging from its fat, pink neck. It stopped at
the alligator's massive feet, looking up at the
minigun-wielding legend. Air Force Gator set his
Croc Blocker down and bent down to pick up the
animal, staring straight into its eyes.

Gator hadn't eaten in days, fueled only by
his need for revenge. Instinctively, the alligator
opened his massive jaw and prepared to eat the
pig whole, bell and all. Without warning, the
small pig belched blue mist directly into the
gaping maw of the alligator.

Dropping the pig, the alligator stumbled
backwards. His vision quickly became blurry as
Air Force Gator felt the power leave his legs.
Before hitting the ground, the heroic alligator's
consciousness left him and his vision went
black.

Blinking his eyes open, Air Force Gator
had no idea if it was hours or days later. He laid
on a cold concrete floor, and looked up to see the
distorted vision of a human with a straw hat.

"I hope you had some sweet dreams about
that dead, big-tittied gal you used to be sweet
on," Van Buren said. "Because now it's time for
your nightmare."

Chapter VIII

July 4, 2013

Alexandria, Virginia

It had been nearly three months since anyone in the United States had heard anything from Air Force Gator. Some assumed he had become a recluse after the death of Trish, reverting to his former life of booze and whores. Many others felt he had committed suicide, his body undiscovered at the bottom of a river or hanging in a cheap motel room. One thing was for certain, though. Van Buren and the Sons of Gustav had taken one American city down, and they planned on striking again. With the heroic alligator out of commission or dead, the American public was beginning to lose hope.

Newspapers and gossip websites ran headlines that predicted Gator's death, but one man never lost hope. Ray "Razor" Connolly was one of only two men that knew where Air Force Gator really was. President Obama was forced to disavow any knowledge of the alligator's location, but Razor was determined to send help to South America. He couldn't prove that Gator was alive on top of that Venezuelan waterfall, but his gut told him that the American hero hadn't left this world yet.

It was Independence Day, a holiday that had always reminded Razor of his best friend, even during the years that they were out of contact. Gator always said it was his favorite holiday, and he spent it each year getting hammered and blowing up watermelons and toilets with M-80s. Sitting on a Boston streetside during a Fourth of July parade, Razor struggled to enjoy it despite his nagging worries about Air Force Gator.

He wiped tears from his eyes as he watched men dressed as Benjamin Franklin and Thomas Jefferson ride floats down the street, throwing candy at children. Keeping his composure was difficult but doable until one float rounded the corner and caused Razor to break down. It was a large alligator balloon, adorned with Air Force Gator's trademark goggles and bomber jacket. Underneath the inflatable creature was a sign that read "A Tribute To A Fallen American Hero."

Wanting to scream and let the world know that Gator wasn't dead, Razor instead balled his fists and vowed to act on his suspicions. He folded up his lawn chair, tossed it in the back of the station wagon he had found in New Orleans, and began the seven-hour drive to Alexandria, Virginia.

Colonel Backlund was dead and President Obama wouldn't be any help given the situation, so Razor had only one man to turn to for help. It wouldn't be easy to convince anyone to help a bartender save an assumed-dead alligator from an evil pig farmer, but Razor was damn sure gonna try to gain an unlikely ally.

Driving the station wagon through the upscale Alexandria suburb, he scanned the ornate houses for the right address. When he finally spotted it, he knew he had found the place. A massive mansion sat on the biggest hill in town, and its driveway was blocked by a massive metal gate.

For a moment, Razor considered buzzing the intercom in an effort to gain entry. Remembering who he was here to visit, he didn't waste his time. He knew there was no way that gate would be opening for him, so he opted to climb it. Years of relative inactivity had left him in worse shape than in his military days, but he could still scale any wall or obstacle like it was nothing.

He crossed over the top of the fence and dropped down to the grass below. Dusting himself off as he stood up, Razor started walking towards the mansion that sat at the end of the long driveway. Knowing that guard dogs were a genuine concern, he kept one hand on the knife at his side. No dogs or other security measures could be seen as he stepped up to the front door of the mansion.

Razor inhaled deeply and exhaled slowly before he knocked, knowing he didn't have an easy sell ahead of him. Raising his fist, he offered two brisk knocks to the oak door. Seconds felt like minutes as he waited for a response. He started to reach for the doorbell, but was interrupted by a voice from inside.

"There's a buzzer on the gate for a fucking reason. Who is this?"

"It's Razor."

Silence followed for several seconds, and then the sound of locks being undone could be heard from inside. The door swung open, and Razor locked eyes with General Layfield for the first time since they witnessed Colonel Backlund's death over eight years ago.

"You've got some nerve, you bartending son of a bitch," Layfield said. "You better have a damn good reason to be standing on my doorstep."

"I wouldn't be here if it wasn't critical, General. You know we've never seen eye to eye, but I know that you're capable of putting personal quibbles aside for the good of this nation."

Layfield stared at the unkempt bartender for a moment before begrudgingly motioning for him to enter the mansion.

"Take your dirty fucking shoes off and sit down," Layfield said. "You need a drink? I sure as fuck do, now that your ugly ass is here."

"I see you're as pleasant a host as you are a superior officer," Razor said. "Yeah, toss me a Bud Light."

"*Toss you a Bud Light?*" Layfield repeated, mockingly. "I'm a god damn general in the United States military...I can afford better booze than that."

"Alright, General Fancypants. Just give me whatever bullshit you've got. We've got more important things to discuss than what we're drinking."

Layfield muted the news on his television, walked to his bar and poured two glasses of wine, then handed one to Razor.

"Wine?" Razor asked. "Do you keep this in your purse?"

"Shut the fuck up and cut to the chase. Why the fuck are you here, and why shouldn't I kick you out of here right now? Last I checked, you haven't been officially active in the military for a longass time."

"It's Air Force Gator."

"That washed-up, junkie son of a bitch again?" Layfield said. "No one has seen or heard from him since New Orleans got sacked. From what I've gathered, most everyone in the country thinks he's dead."

"He's not, General. I know where he went, and I think he's being held hostage."

"That alligator isn't of any use to anyone. Who would be holding him hostage?"

"The Sons of Gustav. After the attack on New Orleans, Gator interrogated their turtle and found out where they were going."

"You idiots interrogated one of those slimy terrorists without the involvement or knowledge of the U.S. military, and you didn't even divulge the information to us? Do you have any idea how deep of a shithole that could put you in?"

"We knew the risks going in," Razor said. "But Gator had that look in his eyes and I knew there was no talking him out of taking matters into his own hands. That stripper was super hot, and he's out for revenge."

"So he's off on some stupid fucking vendetta by himself? If he knew where those assholes were holed up, he could have tipped us off and we would have bombed them back to the stone age!"

"Letting the military take Van Buren and those reptiles out wouldn't be enough for him. Air Force Gator wants to personally kill every last one of those dickweeds."

"That stupid, crazy son of a bitch alligator," Layfield said. "Well where the fuck did he go?"

"Venezuela," Razor said. "They've set up shop on top of the world's biggest waterfall. Neither of us know what the Sons are up to, and that turtle didn't seem high enough on the group's food chain to be wise to the master plan. All we know is that they're down there planning an attack that's even bigger than New Orleans."

"World's biggest waterfall, eh? I'm gonna get the President on the line and we'll make sure it's the world's biggest crater by the end of the week."

"You can't," Razor said. "Gator's there, I know it. That turtle said Van Buren's plan had something to do with 'making an example' out of Gator."

"That's all you're going off of? Something a desperate, terrorist turtle told you during an unauthorized interrogation?"

"We may not have had permission, but that doesn't mean our info is any less valid."

"You're not a military man anymore," Layfield said. "You mean nothing to us, and we've got real work to do. Now that we know where Van Buren and his crocs are, we're sure as fuck not gonna delay it to save a junkie alligator that's probably already dead."

"He's a *national hero*. He saved this country from Gustav's attack. Have you forgotten about that so easily?"

"Get the fuck out of my house, Razor."

"If we don't rescue Gator, the blood is on your hands when the Sons..." Razor stopped midsentence, staring at the muted television screen in the living room. "Look..."

Layfield turned in his chair to face the screen, which displayed a "*BREAKING NEWS: TERRORIST LEADER BREAKS SILENCE*" header over an image neither man expected to see. It appeared to be a malnourished Air Force Gator, binded to a wooden chair with arm restraints. Without saying a word, Layfield grabbed the remote and unmuted the television.

Wearing his trademark straw hat and overalls, Van Buren stepped into the frame holding a newspaper.

"Hello, America," the pig farmer said as he held up the newspaper. "As you can see right here, this ain't no old video. This is today's newspaper, and this is the current state of your precious hero. Take a look at this stupid sumbitch right here."

Air Force Gator's eyes were bloodshot, his face was bruised, and his body had lost significant mass in the months since he was last seen publicly.

"This dumbass Gator is ours, and we're sure as hell not gonna let him die easy. We've had him a few months now, and we've barely even touched him. Plannin' an attack that's gonna shake the core of the United States requires a lot of time and effort, ya see. Thing is, most of the heavy liftin' is done on my little project, so now my men and I can focus on makin' America's favorite alligator see what hell feels like."

Layfield and Razor continued to watch, both men instantly reminded of when they witnessed Colonel Backlund's grisly death live on video. They silently prayed that this wouldn't be a similar situation.

"Reason I'm sendin' this video isn't cause I'm about to kill y'all just yet," Van Buren continued. "I just wanted every one of you reptile-hatin' Americans to know that I've got your hero, and he's gonna spend the remainin' days of his life in the worst fuckin' pain you can even imagine. Once his body shuts down and he's finally rotting in the ground, then and only then will Americans pay for their bigotry at one of their most sacred institutions."

Van Buren turned and stared directly at Air Force Gator's elongated snout.

"We ain't gonna let you die any time soon, Gatah. Not by a long shot, you slimy sumbitch."

"Go to hell, croc sucker," Air Force Gator said as he spit in the face of the pig farmer.

Van Buren ducked out of the camera's frame to wipe the saliva off his face as two guards assaulted Gator. The crocodile guards slammed the butts of their rifles into Air Force Gator's skull until his limp and bloodied body fell to the ground.

"Air Force Gatah's hell begins now, America," Van Buren said as he re-entered the frame. "And once we're done with him, you're all next to feel his pain."

As Van Buren's broadcast ended, Razor grabbed the remote from Layfield's hands and turned the television off.

"So...let's talk about how we get him the fuck out of there," Razor said.

"That was some incredibly convenient timing for you," Layfield said. "But god dammit, you were right."

"They're gonna try to break him. They're going to torture him day and night until he's a shell of his former self. They want America to lose hope in their greatest hero. We can't let that happen."

"I hate to say this," Layfield said. "But I...I want to help you. We need to get that stupid fucking alligator out of that jungle."

"Then make the call. Let's storm Angel Falls with every god damn plane and transport chopper in the Air Force."

"I want to, but do you know how much red tape I'd have to go through? It'd be impossible to get the green light to put hundreds of our men at risk to save one alligator. Even if I did get the go-ahead, he'll probably be tortured to death by the time it takes all those pencil-necked bureaucrats to come to a decision."

"Surely they'd see the importance of this mission. There's no way they've forgotten that Air Force Gator saved this country from the brink of destruction."

"They haven't forgotten," Layfield said. "But they won't care. As much as it pains me to say it, I do care. I hate that fucking alligator, I hate his stupid goggles, I hate his dumb jacket, and his plane looks dumb as fuck. But god dammit, the country loves him. And they need him."

"Then make the call," Razor said. "You know what? You don't even need to involve the government. Set it up so you get me a napalm bomber under the table, and I'll burn that entire area to the ground. Gator's scales are so tough from the GatorAid, he'll be able to escape the flames and we can extract him while the rest of Van Buren's camp burns."

"You want me to help you burn down the rainforest so you can save an alcoholic alligator? Do you know what kind of PR shitstorm that would cause?"

"Not as much as the shitstorm that would come from the US military letting their greatest hero die," Razor said. "You should care a lot more about the US of A's most decorated pilot than you do about some fucking trees."

General Layfield took a long drink of wine, contemplating Razor's offer.

"Fuck the bureaucrats," Layfield said. "They don't have to know shit. Meet me tonight at 3am on the tarmac of Joint Base Andrews. I'll give you a card that will bypass security. Once you're there, I'll toss you the keys to the biggest, most badass napalm bomber we've got. But if shit goes down, you and I never spoke."

"Why would I want to speak to an asshole like you, anyway? We've got plausible deniability."

"Ha ha, fuck face," Layfield said. "I still don't like you, and I still hate that asshole alligator. But you're right. I'll see you on the tarmac tonight."

Chapter IX

July 6, 2013

Auyantepui Mountain, Venezuela

Air Force Gator came to consciousness in a haze, his head pounding with pain and his ears ringing. It was a feeling he'd had so many times before, but it was typically from a bombardment of whiskey shots instead of fists and rifle butts to the skull.

He blinked his eyes open, which proved difficult thanks to the blood that had dried on his eyelids. It was the same blood that currently pooled in his giant mouth and on the cement floor of wherever the fuck he currently was.

Blood meant this probably wasn't a hangover. Sure, he could have gotten into a fight or fallen through a bar window again, but this felt different. Gator had no recollection of the events leading up to his current predicament, but his binded hands were a surefire sign that things hadn't gone well.

A single light bulb dangled from the ceiling, and murky liquid was slowly dripping from pipes in the corner of the room. One door sat to Gator's left, and he heard a squeaking sound approaching it from the hallway outside.

With a metallic creak, the cell door swung open. Pierce, Van Buren's top alligator, pushed a cart into the room. Across the top of the cart laid a white cloth that concealed what was underneath. Gator hoped it was catering of some sort, maybe some boneless chicken or Twizzlers or something. Then again, it probably wasn't catering considering he was certainly being held hostage.

Pierce wheeled the cart next to Air Force Gator and looked at the American hero for the first time since their wordless meeting on the streets of New Orleans on that fateful day in March.

"You don't remember me," Pierce said.

Air Force Gator squinted and tried to make out a face through his blurred vision.

"Who the fuck are you, dickweed?" Air Force Gator managed to mutter before coughing up blood.

"I was driving that car in New Orleans. You know, before you put a Molotov in the butt of one of my friends, made one of the others suck on a flamethrower, and crushed the last one's nuts with a mailbox."

"Haha, oh yeah," Gator said. "That was fucking cool."

"You're a tough son of a bitch, I'll give you that. Then again, all of us alligators are."

"An alligator, eh?" Air Force Gator asked. "Thought Van Buren only had a bunch of dipshit crocs on staff."

"Any and all reptiles are welcome in the Sons of Gustav. It was mostly crocs that signed up, but a few of us gators heeded the call. All of 'em but me died. Plus, you killed our only turtle."

"Well I'll be damned. Sad to see one of my own kind in this shitty operation. I'd have thought any alligator would be too smart to fall for some silver-tongued devil's bullshit rhetoric."

Pierce backhanded Gator hard across his snout, causing small specks of blood to splash against the wall and floor.

"It isn't bullshit," Pierce said. "He's always loved reptiles, and just wants what's best for us. I spent years trying to motivate the other reptiles in my crew, but none of 'em would shape up until Van Buren came along. He's the leader we need."

Footsteps echoed from down the hall as someone approached the chamber. Van Buren slowly stepped into the room, staring daggers into Air Force Gator.

"My ears are burnin'," the pig farmer said. "You gators wouldn't happen to be talkin' about me, would ya?"

"We sure were, Boss," Pierce said. "Air Force Gator here doesn't seem to fall in line with our belief system, believe it or not. He doesn't follow your word the way the Sons and I do. I was just trying to talk some sense into him."

"Naw naw...this gatah's a lost cause. I'm not here to turn our reptilian friend to the right side of history. I'm here to make him suffer, and I want every American to know that their hero has turned into a mere shell of what he used to be."

"I'm going to kill the shit out of you," Air Force Gator said. "You're going to hold me in this room for a while and do a bunch of bullshit to me, and it's probably going to suck, but in the end, I'm absolutely going to murder you."

"Well well..." Van Buren said. "We got us a confident little bastard here, don't we? I can drink to that!"

From under the sheet on the cart, the pig farmer pulled out a bottle of Old Crow whiskey. It was Air Force Gator's favorite. Van Buren unscrewed the cap and took a brief swig.

"Pierce..." Van Buren said as he glanced at his right hand man.

The scarred alligator approached Air Force Gator and used his claws to pry the hero's giant mouth open. Gator struggled to fight it, but Pierce proved too strong. His mouth was wide open as Van Buren began pouring the bottle of Old Crow into Air Force Gator's mouth.

"Drink up, you son of a bitch!" Van Buren said.

The bottle reached its end, and Gator began coughing. Pierce released his grip on the hero's jaw.

"Your..." Gator coughed. "Your plan is to torture me by giving me a bunch of free booze? And my favorite brand? Fuck, man. Maybe I was wrong about you idiots."

"Again!" Van Buren screamed to Pierce, who pried Gator's mouth open.

Another bottle of Old Crow materialized from under the cart, and Van Buren didn't waste any time with a sip of his own. Instead, he shoved the entire bottle down Air Force Gator's throat. The alligator's body dry heaved as it attempted to reject the glass bottle. The large object painfully made its way down Gator's esophagus before resting uncomfortably in his large stomach. Van Buren plunged his boot into the hero's abdomen, causing the Old Crow bottle to shatter within his body.

Air Force Gator coughed and moaned as he felt the glass tear at his organs. He hoped that the booze would take effect quickly and lessen the pain, but his tolerance was high after decades of heavy drinking.

"I'm not dumb enough to think a couple bottles of whiskey are enough to do you in," Van Buren said. "So I got enough booze here to stock a bar for a week. And I bet you know where it's all gonna end up. Right down there in your torn-up ol' guts."

"Sounds like a good Saturday night," Air Force Gator said, attempting to retain his cocky demeanor despite the pain that tore at him inside.

"I'm not tryin' to get you buzzed, Gatah. I'm gonna turn you back into that piece of shit alcoholic that you were before 9/11. You know, the one that couldn't fly a damn plane anymore. The one that your beloved countrymen had given up on and forgotten about. The Air Force Gator that lived in the shadow of his dear ol' dead grandpa. You know, that American war hero that was better than you in every single way."

Van Buren struck a nerve. Air Force Gator had always felt like he had been living in the shadow of Grandpa Gator. Even after all his accomplishments and victories, Air Force Gator still felt inferior to the creator of the Gator Plane.

Rage boiled inside the heroic alligator as he forced himself to dry heave. His throat made gross hacking noises, and it sounded like he was about to cough up some phlegm.

"The fuck are you doin'?" Van Buren asked. "You tryin' to hock a loogie at me?"

"You wish, asshole," Air Force Gator said as he spewed a mouthful of glass and whiskey into the pig farmer's face.

"AAAAAAHHH!" Van Buren screamed as he stumbled away from the chair, clawing at his bloodied face.

Attempting to utilize his GatorAid-enhanced strength, Gator stood upright and struggled against his arm restraints. Before Gator could break free, Pierce sprung into action and kicked him hard underneath the jaw. Air Force Gator flew back and slammed against the concrete wall, his body slowly sinking to the ground.

Picking pieces of glass out of his face, Van Buren reached for the cloth on the cart. He began to wipe away the blood and whiskey that clouded his vision.

"Thanks for deliverin' that sweet chin music, Pierce," Van Buren said. "Dumb fuckin' gator's gonna get it even worse than before now that he tried that bullshit."

Van Buren approached Air Force Gator, still lying on the ground and dazed from the kick.

"Listen, you dumb fuck," Van Buren said. "I don't got time to waste personally feedin' you every single bottle of that booze. Pierce here is gonna hook you up to a god damn IV of the shit, and you'll be an alcoholic piece of trash again before you know it. I can't wait for America to see how far their little hero has fallen."

"It doesn't matter how much whiskey you pump into me," Air Force Gator said. "My cold blood will run red, white, and blue until the day I fucking die."

"We'll see how strong you are after a few days of getting injected with booze," Van Buren said. "Bind him up real good and get that Old Crow pumpin'. We'll let him rot in here for three days and then come back and show this asshole some real pain."

Chapter X

July 9, 2013

Auyantepui Mountain, Venezuela

For 72 long hours, Air Force Gator laid on the cold concrete floor of what had turned into his torture chamber. His arms and legs were bound tight with leather shackles, thick enough to contain even his incredible GatorAid strength.

Next to him on the floor sat a pyramid of ten metal kegs. Each of them had originally been filled with whiskey, but most of it had been drip-fed into Air Force Gator's system at this point. Drunk didn't even begin to describe his current mental state. Even in his wildest, darkest days prior to 9/11, Air Force Gator had never been this incapacitated. Vomit stained the concrete below him as he shifted in and out of consciousness. Even in his more lucid moments, he struggled to remember where he was and what was happening. Memories crept into his brain on a few occasions, but it was never long before he blacked out again and wiped his mental slate clean.

He blinked his eyes open and immediately vomited when he felt the sensation of the room spinning around him. Hearing footsteps approach the chamber for the first time in days, he tried to remember who was holding him hostage and where. Closing his eyes in an attempt to stop the room from spinning, he tried to retrace his steps. His entire life had been a blur since the attack on New Orleans, and the most recent memory he clearly retained was holding the corpse of Trish in his arms. It could have been two weeks ago or two years ago, as his sense of time was long gone.

The metal door swung open, and Van Buren and Pierce stepped into a room that reeked of reptilian vomit. Van Buren switched the light on and laid his eyes on the wreck of an alligator that lay on the floor.

"Hoo-ee!" the pig farmer said. "You look like a pile a' hot garbage. Layin' around in your own filth, just like my little piggies back in Tennessee."

Air Force Gator squinted, his eyes adjusting to the first light he had seen in days. He faintly recognized the man and the alligator in the room with him, but failed to remember who they were or what they wanted.

"Pierce, go ahead and strap him down," Van Buren said.

The scarred alligator wheeled an operating table into the room and lifted the filthy body of Air Force Gator off the stained concrete. Laying the hero on the cold metal of the table, Pierce binded his claws and feet.

Next to the table was another cart with a white cloth over it. Air Force Gator watched as Van Buren removed the cloth to reveal a multitude of operating equipment and torture devices.

"I know you're drunk as fuck right now," Van Buren said. "But even your sloppy ass has got to realize that you're in for some serious pain."

Pierce had always kept his ideals in mind when he committed his crimes, never being a fan of what he deemed unnecessary punishment.

"Looks like you've got everything you need from me," the scarred alligator said as he started to walk out of the room.

"No no no," Van Buren responded. "You're gonna stay right here and watch as this traitor gets what's comin' to him."

Sighing, Pierce walked to the corner of the room and folded his arms. Failing to see how this advanced the reptilian agenda, he bit his tongue as he prepared himself for a difficult display.

Van Buren grabbed a thin bamboo chute from the table and began inspecting it.

"You know, Gatah," Van Buren said. "You're so god damn drunk, I could tell ya just about anything right now and it wouldn't fuckin' matter. Hell, I could even tell you exactly what's I'm gonna do to the good old US of A."

Pierce perked up, simultaneously interested in hearing the plan for the first time and confused as to why Air Force Gator would be the first to know.

"Boss, you sure..." Pierce said before the pig farmer cut him off.

"Fuck yeah I'm sure," Van Buren said. "I want our little alligator buddy to suffer as much as possible. What better way than to let him know exactly what I'm gonna do to his homeland? You see, Gatah...I'm gonna use your own grandpappy's invention to kill dozens of thousands of Americans at one of their most sacred institutions. My boys have been workin' on reverse engineering that Gator Plane of yours for months. About 100 feet from here, I got a hanger with a big-ass zeppelin in it. As I stand here over your drunk-ass body, they're outfitting it with the scale armor that good ol' Grandpa Gator spent years making. I call my baby the *Spirit of Gustav.* That zeppelin's gonna be absolutely invincible, and I'm gonna fly that son of a bitch right to the Super Bowl and bomb the fuck out of it."

Gator was lucid enough to process the toll Van Buren's attack would take on the country. Almost a hundred thousand Americans violently perishing on one of the most celebrated and patriotic days of the year.

"No..." Gator mumbled. "You're insane."

"Naw, I'm pretty fuckin' smart actually. You see, I'm gonna leave you here in this fuckin' jungle. I'll be layin' low until the big game while you're layin' here in your own piss with shakin' hands, just dyin' for that next drink that's never gonna come. You're gonna die here, Gatah. Just a useless, beat-down ol' drunk without a soul in the world. Even if you do manage to make it out of here and get back to the States, you're gonna bum the whole country the fuck out thanks to what a sad sack you are now. Look at ya. Emaciated, drunk as fuck, and you got a stupid beard now. Hell, I kinda want you to wash up on America's shores lookin' like some broke-dick alligator junkie."

"I'm gonna make it back. I'm gonna make it back, and I'll kill you before you get anywhere near the Super Bowl."

"Like hell ya will. You'll wash up on shore and bury your snout in a bottle like you always do. It's in your nature, you piece of shit. Great thing is, you won't even remember where and when I'm gonna strike."

But enough about me," Van Buren continued. "Now I'm gonna torture you for a while.

With the bamboo chute in one hand, Van Buren reached for Gator's claw with the other.

"You know, the Vietcong used to shove these babies under the fingernails of American POWs," Van Buren said. "From everything I've heard, it sounds like it hurts like a bitch."

Lifting Gator's claw, Van Buren jammed the bamboo underneath one of the nails. It was met with rough skin, and Gator didn't flinch.

"Well shit," Van Buren said as he wiggled the bamboo around, hoping to detect some pain from the captive alligator. "Your skin is hard as shit."

"He's an alligator," Pierce said from the corner. "Of course his skin is tough."

"Ok, well fuck that plan," Van Buren said as he tossed the bamboo to the floor. "We'll see how much you like those pretty teeth of yours."

Grabbing pliers from the metal tray, he had Pierce pull Gator's mouth open. For 30 minutes, he attempted to pull the alligator's teeth out one by one. In the end, he was only able to remove three teeth out of the over eighty in Air Force Gator's mouth. Each extraction was met with a slight grunt from the hero, which was significantly less than the screams of agony Van Buren was hoping for.

"God dammit, this is tough," Van Buren said to Pierce. "And there's so many fuckin' teeth in here. This'll take all day, and it doesn't even seem to hurt him much."

"How did you not know that alligators have a shit ton of teeth?" Pierce asked.

"Shut the fuck up, I've got another plan. Even I was hesitant to do this, but it looks like I've got to resort to extreme measures. Get me the bucket and the towel."

Confused, Pierce handed both items to the pig farmer.

"Hoo boy, Gatah," Van Buren said. "You'll be havin' nightmares about this moment for the rest of your stupid life. Pierce, put that towel over this dummy's snout."

Pierce almost spoke up, but thought twice about it and placed the towel over Air Force Gator's mouth.

"Feel what it's like to drown, you son of a bitch!" Van Buren screamed as he slowly waterboarded the heroic alligator. For several minutes, Van Buren poured water directly onto the towel that covered Gator's face. Stopping only to make Pierce refill the bucket, over ten gallons of water had been poured before the pig farmer began hearing a muffled response from the alligator.

"You hear that, Pierce?" Van Buren said. "Listen to that dumbass alligator tryin' so hard to breathe through the water, listen to those gurgles as he feels what it's like to drown."

"Boss..." Pierce said as he pulled the towel away from Gator's face. "He's not struggling to breathe, he's fucking snoring. You gotta know that alligators can stay under water for long as fuck."

"Well god dammit! Outside of killin' that hot stripper, what the fuck do I gotta do to hurt this son of a bitch?"

Until this moment, Pierce had felt an unshakable loyalty to the pig farmer. But now, he felt the need to speak up.

"Boss...when you came down to New Orleans and started up the Sons of Gustav, what was that reason you told me again?"

"It was because I...because I love reptiles, that's why! Remember how I said I grew up loving them and all that? I just wanted to come down to New Orleans and help y'all, that's why."

"So you love reptiles so much, but you had no idea that alligators have tough skin, tons of teeth, and can stay underwater?"

Before Van Buren could fabricate an excuse, a tremor was felt throughout the building.

"Uh...what the fuck was that?" Van Buren asked.

Pierce looked around, confused about what the sudden noise could be. Suddenly, another tremor was felt as an entire wall of the chamber crumbled to the ground. Van Buren and Gustav shielded their eyes as the Venezuelan sunlight poured into the room. Once their eyes adjusted, they caught a glimpse of the entire base engulfed in flames. Crocodiles in lab coats ran around the compound screaming and flailing, fire surrounding them. Above the jail cell, Van Buren heard the sound of a big-ass napalm bomber flying by.

Razor had arrived for his friend.

"Oh, what the *fuck*," Van Buren said as he watched months' worth of work burn to the ground.

"We have to get out of here now," Pierce said. "Let's grab the hostage and get to the zeppelin!"

"Leave the gatah!" Van Buren yelled over the commotion in the base. "Let him die here in these flames!"

Van Buren and Pierce sprinted out of the building that housed Air Force Gator and looked skyward. There, they could see Razor's napalm bomber turning around for another run.

"We gotta stop that son of a bitch before he fucks up the *Spirit of Gustav*!" Van Buren said to Pierce. "Hop in that Gator Plane and take him down!"

Pierce had many talents that benefitted the Sons of Gustav, and his piloting skills were unparalleled in the group. The scarred alligator grabbed the keys from Van Buren and sprinted through flames to reach the legendary plane at the center of the base. In no time at all, he started the engines and performed a vertical takeoff.

As Van Buren sprinted towards the hangar that housed the *Spirit of Gustav*, Air Force Gator attempted to break free of his restraints as flames surrounded him. He wouldn't die in these flames thanks to his ultra-tough skin, but he braced for pain as the fire began to lick at his scales. White-hot flames engulfed the alligator's table as he gritted his teeth, and the leather bindings on his claws began to melt away.

Tatters of the bindings fell to the floor, and Air Force Gator was free. He stood up for the first time in what felt like weeks, and immediately crumpled to the ground. Still deeply intoxicated from the whiskey IV drip, he struggled to stand and steady himself. His first thought was to get to his Gator Plane, but his hopes were dashed as soon as he saw it streak through the sky above him.

Pierce was closing in on Razor, who wasn't expecting much anti-aircraft fire in this makeshift compound. The scarred alligator pressed his clawed thumb down on the same red button that Air Force Gator and his grandfather had pressed so many times before, and the

117

plane's trademark Trident missile erupted forth out of the gaping maw of the aircraft.

Alarms sounded inside the plane, but Razor knew that the large napalm bomber wasn't nimble enough to evade an incoming missile. Half a second before the plane was destroyed in a ball of flame, Razor ejected from the craft. His chute opened, and he dreaded landing in the flaming base below.

Gator saw Razor's chute open, but didn't have time to do anything but stagger away from the flaming base. When he reached the perimeter of the carnage, he noticed that his favorite bomber jacket was ablaze. He spotted a nearby body of water, and summoned whatever strength he had in an effort to reach it. Diving in gracefully, the flames were extinguished and his jacket survived another close call.

Despite being an alligator, Air Force Gator found it difficult to swim for the first time in his life. He had swam while drunk thousands of times, but never in his current physical condition. Assuming that his GatorAid strength would keep him afloat proved to be a bad move, as his captivity and torture at the hands of Van Buren had left him weaker than at any point in his life.

Gator treaded water as he felt himself growing dizzy, and had passed out enough to know that he was in danger of doing it here. A current led the alligator along as he struggled to stay conscious despite his exhaustion. He wouldn't drown if he went underwater for an extended period of time, but now was no time to be passed out. Razor was in danger, and his alligator buddy was the only one that could save him.

Fighting the current, Gator attempted to make it to the edge of the water. Before he did, he realized where he was heading. The river seemed to stop in mid-air, and he heard the crashing of water far below. Air Force Gator was about to plummet off of the largest waterfall in the world.

His situation now more dire than he had realized, Gator felt a surge of adrenaline and continued to fight towards the edge of the river. At the bank sat a large, thick branch that was attached to a fallen tree. He was once again thankful for the long arms that GatorAid had provided, as his prior self would have never been able to reach the branch that protruded into the river.

Upon reaching the branch, Air Force Gator realized just how closely he had come to a terrible situation. Twenty feet downstream, the river turned into a mile-long vertical drop into the rocky waters below. Breathing a sigh of relief, Gator began to pull himself up to safety.

Before he could get his long reptilian torso out of the water, he felt pain shoot through his hand. Glancing up, he saw an old cowboy boot bearing down on his claw.

"Not so fast, you piece of shit."

It was Van Buren. His overalls were covered in dust and burn marks, and a scowl was painted across his face. Above him was a massive zeppelin that was entirely covered in the Gator Plane's impenetrable scale armor.

"How...how is that possible?" Gator asked.

"My scientist crocs got what they needed from your grandpappy's plane," Van Buren said. "Your country has given up on you. No one's gonna have any idea where I am until Super Sunday, but they're damn sure gonna hear from me then. Good news for you is, I'm done fuckin' with you. Goodbye, Air Force Gator."

The pig farmer pulled a pistol from his overalls and pointed it at Gator's face. Just before pulling the trigger, he re-aimed the weapon and fired a round directly into the alligator's bicep.

Air Force Gator groaned as his body fell back into the water. A rope ladder quickly descended from the *Spirit of Gustav* and the pig farmer hopped on. Lifting his pistol into the air, Van Buren began firing into the heavens and cackling as he watched the body of his heroic nemesis reach the edge of the river.

Exhaustion and pain left Air Force Gator's body as he felt himself begin to free fall. Decades of jumping out of planes had made him familiar with this sensation, but the lack of a parachute this time made the adrenaline mix with dread.

The alligator could see the ridge of the plateau extend into the sky as he fell. Above it, he witnessed Van Buren's zeppelin as it escaped the flaming base. Suddenly, the entire massive aircraft disappeared in the blink of an eye.

Gator had seen optic camouflage before, but his free fall didn't give him much time to process what he witnessed. The alligator closed his eyes a moment before his cold body slammed into the waters at the base of Angel Falls.

The impact of the water immediately knocked Air Force Gator out, and the overwhelming force of Angel Falls forced his body further and further down. Out cold, America's hero had no means to fight the current as he was dragged to the depths of the river below.

Chapter XI

July 11, 2013

McKenzie, Tennessee

Dozens of acres of Tennessee farmland had sat undisturbed for over a year, thanks to Van Buren's journey to New Orleans the previous summer. In his absence, dozens of pigs were allowed to roam free on the property, a giant automated feeder dispensing food on a regular basis to ensure they'd stay alive.

On this clear Thursday afternoon, the pigs were startled when they felt the ground beneath their feet part. A few pigs fell into the cavernous chasm, while others scurried away to safer ground. For their entire lives, they had been unaware that they had been standing above what would eventually house their owner's weapon of mass distruction.

Even the pigs on safe ground oinked in fear when the gargantuan, reptile-scaled zeppelin appeared in thin air above them. Disengaging its optic camouflage as it descended, the craft slowly entered the dark hangar that sat below the farmland. Once Van Buren had parked the *Spirit of Gustav* safely underground, the giant grass-covered doors slowly closed above it. A ramp extended from the base of the aircraft, and Van Buren and Pierce emerged through a door.

"Be proud that you were on my baby's maiden voyage," Van Buren said. "The *Spirit*'s gonna be in history books until the end of time."

"I gotta admit, I'm impressed," Pierce said. "Optic camouflage worked without a hitch, and I don't think anything's gonna be able to shoot it down."

"It's unstoppable, my reptilian friend. As great as it is, it ain't movin' until February. This is the part that's gonna test your patience. We lay low for the next seven months, and the feds will drop their guard after the case runs cold. They'll be lookin' for us all over South America and the Caribbean before they ever think to check right under their own noses."

Inside the zeppelin, Razor sat captive in a small cell. He rattled the bars, knowing that the aircraft had reached its destination.

"Sounds like our hostage wants some attention," Pierce said.

"Fuck him. We'll toss him some scraps every once in a while to keep him alive in case we need a bargaining chip, but he ain't goin' nowhere. Maybe we'll strap the dumb sumbitch to the bomb when we drop it on the 50 yard line."

Climbing stairs that led from the hangar to the farmhouse, the two emerged above ground.

"Let's have a little drink to celebrate," Van Buren said as he grabbed two beers from the refrigerator. He sat down on a stool as Pierce sat down at the kitchen table.

"Seems that the end game is proceeding as planned," Pierce said. "But we lost a ton of great reptiles in the last year."

"They died so that future generations of reptiles may live in freedom. Not one perished in vain, Pierce. It may just be me and you now, but the legwork is all done. All we gotta do is fly this baby to that football game in New Jersey and press a button. We strike the greatest blow to the American people in their country's history, and they'll pay for their sins against reptiles."

"I've been thinking about that," Pierce said. "What changes when we drop that bomb? It's not like they're gonna pass a law that lets us vote. We're still not gonna be able to get jobs. If anything, it's just gonna turn the public against us more."

"It's a statement, my friend."

"A statement about what? I joined the Sons because you promised a better future for reptiles. Now that we're in the final stretch, I'm starting to question what this is really about."

"You bite your tongue, gator boy," Van Buren scolded. "We've made it this far. Don't lose sight of the finish line that's right in front of us."

"I was on board from the beginning, but I gotta admit that my confidence got shook back there at Angel Falls."

"Pray tell, what shook ya? The fact that we successfully created the most unstoppable aircraft in military history? The fact that we took America's hero and broke his body and his mind and left him at the bottom of a waterfall? Or was it when we survived a napalm strike and flew it all the way to this farm undetected? I'd love to know what part shook ya."

"Maybe it was the part that proved to me that you don't know shit about reptiles. You supposedly spent your entire life loving and caring for my kind, and you somehow don't know about their tough scales or how many teeth they have? Hell, I watched you try to waterboard a fucking alligator."

Van Buren stood up as he slowly backed towards a kitchen drawer.

"Don't you be gettin' any crazy ideas, boy," Van Buren said as he covertly reached for a butcher knife in the drawer. "I'm on your side...always have been."

The two uncomfortably stared at each other as the pig farmer wrapped his hand around the base of the knife behind him.

"I think I hear our hostage," Van Buren said. "How 'bout you run out there and make sure he ain't tryin' any funny business?"

As Pierce turned around, his eyes caught a glimpse of the positioning of Van Buren's hands. Once the alligator's back was fully turned, the pig farmer raised the knife above his head and lunged forward. Expecting the attack, Pierce quickly shuffled towards Van Buren and delivered his patented superkick to the underside of the farmer's jaw.

Van Buren screamed as he crashed through the kitchen shelving behind him, blood pouring from his mouth. A single tooth dribbled down the front of his chin as he fell to the ground.

"This was never about reptiles!" Pierce said. "That's why you waited so long to tell us about the plan. You're not bombing the Super Bowl to help reptiles, you're doing it to protest all the pigs that they slaughter every year to make those footballs. Not to mention all those hot dogs and other crap at the concessions that comes from your precious little piggies. This isn't a war on humanity...you used our mistreatment at the hands of humanity to fuel your own war against professional football and pork eaters."

"What?" Van Buren asked as he sat on the floor and wiped blood off his chin. "No. No, that's...huh. Way off base. Nah, I just want to kill a shitload of Americans."

"Buy why? What's your beef with humans if the entire founding of the Sons was based on a lie?"

"You wanna know why, you stupid reptile son of a bitch?" Van Buren asked as he reached into the neck of his flannel shirt. He pulled out a bloody pair of dog tags. "I risked my life fightin' for this god damned country. Uncle Sam gives me a fuckin' Bronze Star in Desert Storm, then he gives me a dishonorable discharge and tells me to fuck off."

"They don't give dishonorable discharges for nothing, Van Buren."

"Well they did here!"

"No they didn't."

"Shut the fuck up, you god damn gator. What do you know about war? I was stationed up in a farm house with my squadron, and we had to keep an eye out for scud transports every night for two weeks. Three times, Iraqi snipers fired into that house. I lost two of my friends in that hellhole. You have any idea what it's like fightin' off Iraqis in a farmhouse?"

"You were stationed in a farm?" Pierce asked.

"That's right."

"You fucked a pig, didn't you?"

"Gaaaaaaawwd dammit!" Van Buren screamed as he summoned the strength to stand. He ran across the kitchen floor, lowered his shoulder and tackled Pierce. "Who the fuck told you?"

"No one, you idiot!" Pierce yelled as he pried the pig farmer's hands off his neck. "It was an assumption!"

Punching Van Buren in the face, he rolled the pig farmer onto his back. Next to them on the floor sat the butcher knife that had been dropped in the initial skirmish. Pierce wrapped his claw around the knife and raised it into the air.

"Nighty night, pig fucker," Pierce said as he prepared to plunge the knife between Van Buren's eyes.

Just before lowering the knife, the scarred alligator heard a noise directly above him.

Oink.

Before Pierce had time to react, the pig belched the same blue mist that knocked Air

Force Gator out in Venezuela. The scarred alligator struggled to maintain consciousness, but his body was on the floor in seconds.

Still bleeding from the mouth, Van Buren stood up and dusted himself off.

"That's a good boy," Van Buren said as he petted the pig's head in a kind of creepy manner. "Trained ya well."

The pig farmer looked down at Pierce, who was lying in the floor in his last seconds of consciousness.

"The American people are gonna pay for their country's crimes," Van Buren said. "Ain't no reason a war hero like myself deserves the way I was treated just 'cause I love me a pig."

"No, that's a perfectly good reason to discharge someone," Pierce mumbled as he slowly passed out. "It's super weird and you're lucky they didn't lock you up, you..."

"You what, boy?" Van Buren said. "What's that you were gonna say?"

Pierce's eyes closed before he could accurately call Van Buren a creepy piece of shit. Van Buren grabbed the alligator by the feet and began dragging him towards the *Spirit of Gustav*.

When Pierce came to, his vision was reduced to a small circle that peered off into what appeared to be an endless horizon of clouds and water. He struggled to move, but realized his entire body was surrounded by what felt like iron. Suddenly, Van Buren's voice could be heard through what sounded like a loudspeaker.

"Good mornin', Pierce! I know you weren't too involved in the making of this beautiful zeppelin, but I wanna tell you a little about the *Spirit of Gustav.* Ya see, it's not just for droppin' that bomb on the Super Bowl. It's ready to defend itself against any Air Force assholes in case they catch wind of my little plan. I got turrets, anti-air missiles, and even a big-ass cannon.

My boy, I wanted to give you the honor of bein' the first to test out the *Spirit*'s cannon. It's the least I can do since you won't be able to join me in February for its big debut. Goodbye, Pierce. Say hi to that shark that gave you that dumbass scar if you see him."

Realizing what the pig farmer was about to do, Pierce scrambled in an attempt to exit the front of the cannon. He was too late.

Gunpowder boomed as the alligator's body was propelled out of the cannon. In mid-air, Pierce came to the realization that Van Buren must have flown out to the middle of the ocean to dispense of his former right hand man. As the alligator saw the *Spirit of Gustav* disappear into the distance, he held up both claws and raised his middle fingers. Seconds later, his body crashed into the Atlantic Ocean.

The *Spirit of Gustav* activated its optic camouflage and headed back to the pig farm in Tennessee, where it would sit until Super Bowl Sunday.

Chapter XII

December 25, 2013

Washington, D.C.

It was Christmas night in the medical wing of Joint Base Andrews. As he had every night for the last five months, General Layfield sat silently in the medical wing of the facility. Even in the coma center, it was a surprisingly quiet night. Christmas lights around the window were the only thing illuminating the room, but Layfield knew there was nothing he needed to see. Twisting his seventh glass of wine back and forth between his fingers, he stared at the wounded hero that lay in front of him.

Air Force Gator had been in a coma since late July. After Razor's failed attack on the Angel Falls base, the military mobilized in an attempt to catch Van Buren before he escaped. All they found was piles of charred crocodile corpses, dozens of demolished buildings, and more importantly, an intact Gator Plane.

Unfortunately, they quickly learned that the owner of the Gator Plane wasn't in nearly as good of shape as the aircraft. He had washed up on shore near the river, and a small village of locals had been caring for the alligator ever since his plunge off the world's largest waterfall.

Air Force pilots flew the Gator Plane back to Joint Base Andrews and stored it in an unused hangar. The legendary alligator pilot himself was loaded onto an extraction helicopter, where Coast Guard medics tended to him on the flight back to D.C. Nothing but the alligator's vital signs offered any kind of response. He hadn't eaten a vegetable in decades, but he had become one for all intents and purposes.

Most of the wounds from his torture and fall had healed at this point. Being bedridden for five months helped heal the hero's broken femur, ribcage, pelvis, and lower snout. A few new scars were present on the American legend's face, but they blended in with the dozens of others that he had amassed over the years in military conflicts and barroom brawls.

His wounds may have healed, but evidence of his treatment in Venezuela was painfully apparent. The alligator was emaciated, his leathery skin sinking deep into his face. A large beard extended from his jaw, draping over the hospital blanket.

Most concerning of all was the loss of his trademark giant muscles. Even before the GatorAid made his biceps absurdly gigantic, he was known for having one of the most impressive physiques in the military. On this Christmas night, Layfield stared at a mere shell of a legend. His arms maintained their long length, but any hint of their former power had faded away.

The general had always hated the alligator, but he couldn't deny his importance to the country. Ever since the raid on Angel Falls, military intelligence had gone completely cold on

Van Buren's location. It didn't help that the pig farmer had repeatedly sent the news media reminders that an attack was looming. Many of these videos featured Razor, held captive in a cage surrounded by belching pigs. No matter how much time analysts spent attempting to narrow down Van Buren's location, they never got any closer to finding him.

Under normal circumstances, Layfield and military intelligence would chalk these repeated threats up to mere saber-rattling. However, the pig farmer's devastating assault on New Orleans proved that he had the means to pull off a devastating strike. It was just a matter of time until Americans lives were at risk once again, but no one had the slightest clue what to expect.

Layfield looked at the clock and realized it was almost midnight. He had been sitting in this hospital room for five hours, and Air Force Gator hadn't moved an inch. It was par for the course at this point, but it always depressed the general to have to leave America's hero each night.

Setting his wine glass down, Layfield stood over Gator's hospital bed.

"Merry Christmas, you old son of a bitch," the general said to Air Force Gator's unconscious body. "Wake up soon. First beer's on me when you do."

As Layfield turned to walk away, he paused when he heard brief snorting sounds from the bed. His jaw dropped as he witnessed Air Force Gator's eye slowly opening.

"Fuck...you..." Air Force Gator said through clenched teeth, his first words since being airlifted from Venezuela. "I'm drinking you under the table, and you're paying for it all."

"Oh my god, Gator!" Layfield screamed as he approached the bed. He bent down and attempted to hug the American hero.

"What the fuck?" Gator said as he pushed Layfield away. "Get off my dick, Layfield."

"I'm sorry, Gator...I'm just shocked. I've been here every night hoping for this moment. The country needs you."

"You've spent every night watching me sleep?" Gator said. "That's fucking weird. You didn't have anything else to do with your time?"

"Look, that doesn't matter. All that matters now is that you tell us what happened while you were down there in Venezuela. You spent two months face-to-face with that pig fucker, and we need to stop him before he attacks again. Now tell me...what do you remember? Tell me everything."

Gator closed his eyes for a few moments, trying his best to conjure up any memories of Van Buren's plan.

"Fuck, man," Gator said. "Venezuela? Honestly, I don't really remember what the fuck happened down there. Everything that happened after that hot stripper died is a blur."

"You mean to tell me you don't remember anything that happened after the attack on New Orleans?"

"I think I killed a turtle or something."

"God dammit," Layfield said. "Get yourself together. I'm gonna tell the doctors you're awake, and I'm coming back tomorrow with a camera. You're gonna need to tell us everything you know, and we're gonna find and kill that son of a bitch."

Frustrated, Layfield turned to walk out of the room.

"Wait..." Air Force Gator said under his breath. "There is one thing."

Layfield stepped closer to the hospital bed.

"Closer..." Air Force Gator whispered, seemingly in pain from the mere act of talking.

Once Layfield took another step towards the alligator, he was struck in the testicles by the backside of Air Force Gator's claw.

"AGH!" Layfield yelled as he doubled over. No matter how many times the alligator nut tapped him, the general never expected it. "You son of a bitch! I'll see you tomorrow."

Air Force Gator let out a huge belly laugh as Layfield awkwardly left the room, his hands gingerly cradling his aching scrotum.

Even though it was midnight, Air Force Gator couldn't sleep. It was the first time his eyes had been open in months, and he spent the early morning hours attempting to retrace the steps that ended with him falling into a coma.

Staring in the bathroom mirror, Gator was shocked to see what months of inactivity had done to him.

"God dammit," Gator said as he pulled at his long, stringy beard. "I look like some asshole that listens to Bon Iver."

Looking around for any kind of cutting utensil, Air Force Gator came up short. Desperately wanting to rid himself of his shitty beard, he reached up and gripped it with both claws.

"*Fuuuuuuuck*," Gator moaned as he began to pull at the scraggly hair. His chin and cheeks flared up with pain as the beard was ripped from his face.

Now that his stupid beard was gone and he looked like a respectable alligator again, Air Force Gator focused his attention on the state of his body. He pinched his bicep, and was shocked to be met with flappy skin in the place of his usual muscles.

Without thinking, Gator slammed his fist through the glass of the mirror, shattering it into a million pieces. Leaving the bathroom with bloody knuckles, he looked up to see a pipe running across the ceiling of his hospital room.

Air Force Gator decided there was no time like the present to begin his road to redemption, and he jumped up and grabbed the bar. Despite how difficult his lack of strength made it, the alligator did pull-up after pull-up until the sun rose and peeked through the windows.

When Layfield walked into the hospital room the next morning, the American hero was still doing pull-ups.

"This is promising," Layfield said.

"Fuck off," Air Force Gator said as he dropped off the bar and stretched his arms. "I'm not doing this for you. I'm doing this so I don't look like some latte-sipping pussy."

"That's best for everybody," Layfield said. "Sit down. Now that you've had a night to readjust to being alive again, it's time to get down to brass tacks."

"This is the first time I've ever been excited to hear you talk. Start movin' your pie hole, dickweed. What happened down there in Venezuela?"

"We found you unconscious in a small village. You had fallen off Angel Falls after being tortured for months. We airlifted you and the Gator Plane back to D.C."

"The Gator Plane is here?" Air Force Gator said. "Thank god...I was worried that cocksucker pig farmer kept it. What about the Croc Blocker?"

"It's safely sitting in the cockpit of your Gator Plane. Your toys are just fine, Air Force Gator. What we're worried about is you. It seems that your treatment in Venezuela and ensuing coma has caused the GatorAid's effects to dissipate. I don't know if you've seen a mirror lately, but you're not exactly the physical specimen you used to be."

"I can still kick the shit out of you. And don't worry, I plan on getting right back to where I used to be."

"We might not have time for you to do things the natural way," Layfield said as he pulled up a briefcase from under his chair. "We need you in top condition right away."

Opening the briefcase, Layfield revealed several syringes filled with neon orange liquid.

"GatorAid," Air Force Gator said. "Why the fuck do you have that?"

"You know why. The doctor will be in here this afternoon to administer the dose. We'll get those muscles back in no time at all."

Gator stared at the chemical, remembering how good it felt when he emerged from the infected waters near Crocodile Rock. After thinking about it for a few seconds, he angrily slammed the case shut with his claw.

"No," Air Force Gator said. "Grandpa Gator didn't need any help to be great. He was naturally brilliant, naturally talented. If I'm ever gonna live up to my namesake, I'm gonna do it the right way. I'm not about to go down in history as the Jose Canseco of alligators."

"Well, you'd have to rat out all of your friends to make a quick buck to do that," Layfield said.

"No. I'm Air Force Gator, dammit. I'm gonna be the greatest soldier this country has ever seen, and I'm doing it all myself. You and your shortcuts can suck it."

Not waiting for a response from Layfield, and with no interest in hearing the opinions of some eggheads in labcoats, Air Force Gator grabbed his bomber jacket and stormed out of the hospital. He swung by the liquor store to grab a crate of 40s, and went straight to the military's training facility.

For over a month, Air Force Gator spent day and night drinking Mickey's and slowly regaining his amazing strength. He pulled tractor trailers with ropes. He did awesome one-handed alternating push-ups. He spent hours wailing on a punching bag while inspiring music echoed through the gym.

He was ready. He didn't know when or where he'd have the chance to get his hands on Van Buren again, but he was making damn sure he'd be ready when he did.

February 2, 2014

Washington, D.C.

Over a month since Air Force Gator woke from his coma, little of his memory had returned. Hours upon hours were spent talking to military doctors, psychologists, and intelligence officers, but nothing that pointed towards Van Buren's current position. His last broadcast to the media ended with a cryptic message about it being his last, leading the FBI to believe his strike was looming.

No longer in the hospital, Air Force Gator had moved to the nearby barracks. Layfield spent entire days asking questions as Air Force Gator did push-ups, bench pressed hundreds of pounds, and enthusiastically thumbed through titty magazines. Some vague memories of his time in Venezuela had resurfaced, but they typically revolved around his treatment rather than the pig farmer's words.

With presumably little time to act before Van Buren's strike, the situation was becoming more dire. Today, Layfield found himself once again making the walk down the barracks hall towards Air Force Gator's room. As usual, the entirety of Lynyrd Skynyrd's *Nuthin' Fancy* album could be heard blasting on repeat from inside the alligator's room.

The general stepped into the doorway and saw Air Force Gator punching away at a heavy bag. Despite becoming frustrated at the alligator being unable to provide intelligence, Layfield was genuinely impressed by the speed in which he had recovered from his coma. Gator was super huge again, and looked as ferocious and hungry as ever as he wailed away on the bag with hooks, roundhouse kicks, and tail swipes.

"Well shit, Gator," Layfield said. "You're looking tougher than a two dollar steak."

"Fuck yeah I am," Gator said while uppercutting the bag. "Just because I can't remember what that pencil dick was telling me doesn't mean I can't still fuck him up."

"Good to know. Hopefully we can put those skills to good use at some point, and hopefully it's before more Americans have to die."

The general pulled up a chair and sat down.

"I can't stay all day. Just swinging by again to see if anything else came back to you."

"Actually, a little bit did," Gator said as he stopped punching the bag. "I remember that there was another alligator there. I killed a shit ton of crocs, but there was still one alligator alive, and he seemed important."

"Good, good," Layfield said as he handed Gator his daily request of 30 bottles of Bud Light. "Any names or information?"

"No, but there was this other thing...I can't remember if it was real or a dream I had at some point. I was fucked up in some water, and I swear there was some big fucking blimp or zeppelin or something. Last thing I have any memory of whatsoever is seeing that redneck climb up into it as it floated away."

"That son of a bitch has his own zeppelin? That's gotta be how he's planning on delivering his bomb or whatever the fuck it is."

"Yeah, it was fucking huge. But there's some weird shit that makes me think that it might have been a dream or a hallucination or some bullshit."

"Any information at all is helpful."

"It's gonna sound crazy, but I thought the zeppelin was covered in scale armor. That's dumb as fuck though, because the only thing that's ever had scale armor is the Gator Plane."

"Christ, what the hell are we dealing with here?" Layfield asked.

141

"That's not all. I think it fucking disappeared. The whole big-ass thing, just...gone. I know I wasn't in the best mental state at the time, but I fucking remember a blimp covered in scales disappearing as that pig farmer flew away."

"This is great information," Layfield said. "We can use this. I'm gonna get intel on this right away and see if we've noticed any unauthorized zeppelin traffic in recent months."

"That's all for now, though. Nothing else is coming to mind. Just a blur of stupid torture and shitty food."

Layfield shook Air Force Gator's claw.

"Little by little, we're getting somewhere," Layfield said. "We'll catch this son of a bitch. I'll check back in tomorrow."

As Layfield grabbed his jacket and prepared to leave, a knock came on the door.

"I'll get that, I'm heading out anyway," the general said.

When he opened the door, a Pizza Hut delivery man was standing there with a gigantic box.

"I've got 10 stuffed crust pizzas and two boxes of boneless WingStreet wings for an Air Force Gator," the delivery man said.

"Holy shit, Gator," Layfield said. "Having people over for the big game?"

"Nope, just..." Gator stopped midsentence as his eyes widened. His claw involuntarily lost its grip on his bottle of Bud Light. Before the bottle even crashed to the floor, memories flooded the alligator's tiny little alligator brain.

"I'm gonna fly that son of a bitch right to the Super Bowl and bomb the fuck out of it," Van Buren's voice echoed in Air Force Gator's memory.

The bottle of Bud Light shattered on the floor, sending glass shards and delicious, affordable alcohol everywhere.

"That butthead is gonna bomb the Super Bowl," Air Force Gator said.

Layfield barely had time to process the sentence before the alligator had grabbed his keys, thrown on his bomber jacket, slammed another Bud Light, and ran out the door.

The general pulled out his phone and began to dial the President as the unmistakable sound of the Gator Plane roared above the building.

Chapter XIII

February 2, 2014

East Rutherford, New Jersey

Over a hundred million viewers tuned into the live broadcast, raising their beers and devouring pizza from the comfort and safety of their own homes. Eighty thousand Americans filled MetLife Stadium for Super Bowl XLVIII, completely unaware that their ticket also served as a front-row seat to the largest attempted terror attack in history.

Less than half a mile away, a manic Van Buren was behind the controls of his giant zeppelin. Razor was still in his cage, surrounded by dozens of pigs. One of the pigs peered out the window of the aircraft, and began defecating everywhere in fear.

"Aw, Christ," Razor groaned.

"Haha, yeah," Van Buren laughed. "They get the shits real bad the second they realize we're above the clouds. Scares the dickens out of 'em."

More and more pigs began staring out the windows of the zeppelin, each beginning to crap everywhere in fear.

"This is fucking gross, you dickwad,"

Razor said.

"Patience. Some pig shit'll be the least of your worries in a few minutes. I want you to watch as the whole god damn Super Bowl blows up, and then I'm gonna feed you to those little piggies. They'll eat ya real slow. Air Force Gator's gonna hear about how I ruined Super Sunday by blowin' up his countrymen at his favorite event, but the real kicker ain't gonna come until he learns about you. In less than one year, I'll have killed his hot stripper girlfriend, blown up the Super Bowl, and fed his best friend in the whole world to some fuckin' pigs. If that ain't enough to ruin that alligator for good, I don't know what is."

Razor wondered if Air Force Gator had it in him to save the day like he had done so many times before. For the months that Razor had been held captive, he had no access to the outside world in any form. News agencies had broken the story about Air Force Gator's return from Venezuela and subsequent recovery, but the alligator's best friend was still in the dark.

With a crazed grin, Van Buren was affixing parachutes to each of his pigs.

"Now listen here, sweeties," the farmer said to the pigs. "Y'all gonna be real scared when you start fallin', but you'll be safe on the ground. As soon as those people see the *Spirit*, they're gonna be scramblin' to get out of that stadium."

The pigs stared wordlessly at their owner.

"You all remember your jobs, right?" Van Buren asked as he held up a crudely-drawn picture. It consisted of several pigs blocking a doorway as stick figures were engulfed in flames behind them. "You find all the exits and block 'em up real good. That way, everyone's stuck in there and they're goin' straight to hell. Not my darlins, though. Y'all goin' straight to piggy heaven for this."

The farmer pulled a lever, and a cargo door opened in the rear of the zeppelin. Van Buren began heaving the crap-covered pigs one by one out into the sky. Now super scared, they started pooping so much more.

It was the end of the second quarter. As the Green Bay Packers and Pittsburgh Steelers trotted off the field and towards their locker rooms, an army of roadies and concert techs swarmed the stage to prepare for the AC/DC concert at halftime.

Before most fans could even stand up to make a quick concession run or trip to the pisser, a nightmare appeared above them. Seemingly from thin air, the massive, green, scale-covered *Spirit of Gustav* appeared in the sky above the parking lot. Murmurs were heard throughout the crowd, with many suspecting it was part of an elaborate halftime performance.

At almost the exact moment the zeppelin appeared, President Obama appeared on the stadium's giant television screens. The words *EVACUATION ORDER* appeared under his image.

"Football fans, this is an urgent message from your president," Obama said. "We have just received word that noted terrorist Van Buren is en route to MetLife Stadium in a large aircraft, most likely transporting a weapon of mass destruction. As a result, I'm ordering an evacuation of the stadium and any residences within five miles immediately."

Fans in attendance were only able to hear the beginning words of the message, as panic and screaming erupted amongst them as soon as the headline had appeared onscreen.

"TRY AND RUN, YOU STUPID ASSHOLES!" Van Buren screamed through the *Spirit*'s powerful intercom system. "I'll flatten a square mile with the bombs I got on this baby! Ain't no chance in hell any of you gonna escape this payload!"

Most of his pigs were still in mid-air, many of them still crapping. Van Buren's sights were squarely set on the stadium that he was quickly approaching, and he never expected what was arriving behind him at hundreds of miles per hour.

Soaring through the sky, the Gator Plane

arrived on the scene. Its gaping mouth wide open, it flew directly through several floating pigs. Blood and pig entrails stained the giant alligator head that made up the body of the legendary aircraft.

"Guess who's back, cocksucker!" Gator screamed as he approached the *Spirit*.

The American hero grabbed his flight stick and pressed down hard on the big red button. A Trident erupted from the gaping mouth of the Gator Plane and quickly split into three homing missiles. All three adjusted and sped directly towards Van Buren's zeppelin.

An excited grin crept across Air Force Gator's face as he prepared for his missiles to strike. One by one, they connected with the *Spirit of Gustav* and exploded in a ball of flames.

Gator's excited grin quickly left his snout as the smoke cleared. The Gator Plane's trademark attack hadn't left a single scratch on the pig farmer's weapon of mass distruction.

"Aw, fuck," the alligator said as he slammed his claw on the plane's console. He sped underneath the *Spirit* and attempted another approach. Noticing that the only part of the zeppelin not covered in scales was the metal carriage that contained the cockpit, he decided that the best option would be to ram it from the side.

149

As Gator repositioned himself in preparation for the strike, Van Buren glanced out of the side windows of his zeppelin.

"Looks like the slimy son of a bitch is alive after all," Van Buren said. "I guess the so-called legend finally decided to show up."

"Your time is up," Razor said from his cage.

"Is it, now?"

Van Buren ran to the cockpit's controls as the Gator Plane rushed towards him. Pressing a few buttons, the pig farmer activated the *Spirit*'s defense systems.

Inside the Gator Plane, the alligator braced for impact as the zeppelin's turret fire ricocheted off of the huge alligator head that he was sitting in. Just before impact, the zeppelin's cannon picked up on Gator's heat signature and readied itself for its new target.

"*BOOM,*" Van Buren whispered to himself.

With a thundering crack, a 1,500 pound cannonball exploded out of the cannon's chamber. A mere second before Air Force Gator would have crashed into the zeppelin, the ball slammed into the legendary plane that Grandpa Gator built.

Still intact, the Gator Plane was thrown wildly off course. It went into a sharp descent, speeding towards the very stadium that Van

Buren was targetting. Crashing directly onto the 50 yard line, the craft became embedded several feet into the field's grass.

Gator was rattled in the crash, but the nearly indestructible exterior of the Gator Plane had prevented any serious injuries. He fumbled with the cockpit console for a few moments before recognizing that the plane was in no way capable of taking off. He kicked the door open and slowly crawled out of the wreckage. Glancing around, he saw that much of the crowd had been unable to escape the stadium. This was due to a lack of sufficient exits and general panic, howver, not the crap-covered pigs that had abandoned (or never arrived at) their designated posts. Instead of following Van Buren's plan, they were now aimlessly wandering around the parking lot as football fans attempted to run to their cars.

Looking up from the center of the field, Air Force Gator wondered if this was really the end. Now almost directly over the center of the field, the *Spirit of Gustav* was opening its bomb bay doors. In mere seconds, its payload would be deployed and the stadium and surrounding area was bound to be flattened.

With no other available approach, Gator reached into the downed plane and pulled out the Croc Blocker. Heaving the minigun up, he aimed it directly at the *Spirit*. Inside Gustav's decapitated head, the barrel began spinning. A steady stream of gunfire began exiting the chamber, but its ammo either didn't reach the zeppelin or impotently bounced off of its scaly exterior.

"Goodbye, everyone! It's time to meet your maker!" Van Buren screamed as he prepared to press the button that would drop the *Spirit*'s bombs.

Before pressing his finger down, Van Buren spotted another aircraft in the sky above the stadium. A small Skyhawk plane flew perpendicular to the zeppelin's path, and a banner trailed behind it. Van Buren squinted as he read the large block letters.

"LICK MY ASSHOLE, ASSHOLE."

Recognizing it was Air Force Gator's catchphrase confused him more, as the American hero was visible on the 50 yard line below him. Now speeding directly towards him, Van Buren was able to catch a quick glimpse of the pilot.

Pierce sat behind the cockpit glass, gritting his teeth as he flew directly into the carriage that held Van Buren and Razor. The propellor of the small craft was crushed and flew off as the plane blasted through the zeppelin's controls and Van Buren's body. Dragging the pig farmer down with it, the small plane plummeted to the field below. It struck the grass only 20 feet from Air Force Gator, and Van Buren's body was tossed further down the field.

With its console destroyed, the *Spirit of Gustav* slowly began a nose dive into the upper section of MetLife Stadium. As it softly collided with the seats, Razor's cage slid out and shattered on the concrete steps. Free for the first time in months, he began sprinting down to field level.

There, Pierce gingerly pulled himself out of the downed Skyhawk. The scarred alligator glanced at his bloodied former boss, still breathing and moaning as he lay on the football field. Walking over to Air Force Gator, Pierce extended his claw.

"I'm sorry," the scarred alligator said. "I was wrong to follow this maniac. He made me think I'd be helping reptiles like us if I joined him, but killing Americans isn't the way to help anybody."

Air Force Gator stared at his former captor.

"I don't know, man," Gator said. "You guys really fucked me up back in Venezuela. Ah, fuck it. You just saved my ass and fucked up that dickbreath over there."

They both laughed as they glanced at Van Buren, who was gasping and losing blood at a rapid pace. Air Force Gator gripped Pierce's cold claw hard as the two reptiles shook hands.

"God, look at this dipshit," Gator said.

"Tell me about it," Pierce responded. "Dude fucked a pig. I bet even his dick is like a tiny, curly little pig tail."

Air Force Gator laughed.

"I think you and me are gonna get along fine," the hero said. "Even if you did steal my line up there."

"I always thought it was a pretty good one, honestly," Pierce said. "Although I've always wondered...is that just some cool thing you say or do you actually make people lick your asshole before you kill them?"

"Well..." Air Force Gator said as he looked back at Van Buren. "I guess now's as good a time as any to start backing up that threat."

Van Buren coughed up blood and spoke for the first time since the crash.

"What?" the bloody farmer said. "I heard that. You two have done enough now, ya hear? You keep that slimy alligator butthole away from me!"

As the two alligators approached the dying pig farmer, he flailed with weak, injured arms and legs in an effort to prevent their plan.

"I think we're gonna have to make a wish," Air Force Gator said as he grabbed one of Van

Buren's arms.

"I wish we both get laid tonight thanks to this," Pierce said as he grabbed the other.

Both alligators pulled as Van Buren's arms separated from his torso at the shoulder. Blood poured out onto the football field as the farmer squirmed and kicked. Each alligator grabbed one of his legs.

"We're getting laid for sure," Air Force Gator said. "So my wish is that the first round of shots is on you."

The two alligators pulled hard, and Van Buren's legs were torn from his body. Tossing the limbs aside, Air Force Gator stood above the head of his dying nemesis.

"Aw no," Van Buren pleaded as Gator slowly lowered his body inch by inch. "No no no...you keep that god damn butthole away from me! Seriously, now. You can't be doin' that."

"*Lick my asshole, asshole*," Gator said as Pierce clapped his claws.

Gator squatted down and thrust his butthole right onto the pig farmer's face.

"OH MY GOD THAT'S SO GOD DAMN GROSS!" the farmer screamed as his limbless body attempted to squirm away. "OH GOD GET THAT SLIMY ALLIGATOR BUTTHOLE OFFA MY FACE!"

Air Force Gator laughed and Van Buren

155

screamed and pleaded for several minutes.

"Alright, this is making my thighs sore," Gator said as he stood up. "I've had my fun."

Gator took a few steps away as Van Buren began to spit and dry heave.

"Oh, one more thing," Air Force Gator said, his back to the dying farmer. "Looks like you got something on your face."

When Air Force Gator turned around, Van Buren saw that he now had the Croc Blocker in hand. The alligator pointed the barrel of the minigun directly at the pig farmer's head and held the trigger down.

Thousands of rounds erupted from the disembodied head of Gustav, and Air Force Gator didn't let go of the trigger until there was nothing left of Van Buren's head. All that remained above the limbless torso was a huge, brain matter-filled hole in the grass of MetLife Stadium.

High-fiving above what remained of the pig farmer's torso, the two alligators decided that their work here was done. As they turned to exit the stadium, they heard a helicopter descend from above.

A black helicopter with the seal of the President of the United States landed near the site of the carnage. Fans that hadn't been able to escape the stadium yet started to realize that the threat had been eliminated, and they watched as

Barack Obama and Joe Biden stepped onto the field.

"Air Force Gator, you've done it again," the president said as he offered a salute.

"All in a day's work," the alligator said as he returned the salute.

"You salty old son of a bitch," Joe Biden said as he hugged the heroic alligator. "God, I can't imagine the kinda tail you're gonna be able to pull tonight. Mind if I join?"

Razor sprinted up to the group, breathless after running through the stadium to reach the field.

"Hell yeah you can join," Air Force Gator said. "But I'm not driving your drunk ass home again. Oh, and another thing. My old buddy Razor here and my new buddy Pierce are gonna join us."

"Every red-blooded American can join us tonight," President Obama said. "The first time we tried to celebrate Air Force Gator Day, that bloody pile of stumps over there ruined it. I say tonight's the night we do things right."

"I'd be honored, Mr. President," Air Force Gator said. "Plus, ol' scarface here is buying the first round."

"Fuck yeah, free booze!" Biden exclaimed as he raised his hands above his head.

Air Force Gator, Ray "Razor" Connolly,

Pierce, Vice President Joe Biden, and President Barack Obama all turned and exited the stadium, laughing and mocking crap-covered pigs in the parking lot on the way to the nearest watering hole.

America was safe again.

Acknowledgments

Writing this stupid book was a hell of a lot of fun, and I want to thank the following people for their support during the process:

- Michael Nevins for once again providing cover art that's way too good for a book this dumb
- Bryan Vore, Jeff Cork, and Erin Towner for their help in proofreading
- The Game Informer community for continuing to encourage my idiotic behavior
- Everyone at Game Informer for putting up with me talking about Air Force Gator all the time. Everyone except Joe Juba.
- Everyone that left reviews (positive or negative) on Amazon or elsewhere on the internet. I was able to remedy the two main criticisms of the first book (not long enough and not dumb enough) thanks to feedback from readers.
- You know what? Fuck it. Thanks, Jose Canseco. There's absolutely no reason that you should have responded to my Twitter trolling by actually writing the foreword to my book, but you did. I hope that your dumb ass helps me make thousands of dollars.

Of course, thanks to everyone that took the time to read Air Force Gator 2: Scales of Justice.